SEND FOR PAUL TEMPLE

Francis Durbridge

WILLIAMS & WHITING

Cover design by Timo Schroeder

9781912582518

Williams & Whiting (Publishers)
15 Chestnut Grove, Hurstpierpoint,
West Sussex, BN6 9SS

Titles by Francis Durbridge published by Williams & Whiting

1) The Scarf (tv serial)
2) Paul Temple and the Curzon Case (radio serial)
3) La Boutique (radio serial)
4) The Broken Horseshoe (tv serials)
5) Three Plays For Radio Vol 1
6) Send For Paul Temple (radio serial)

Murder at the Weekend (rediscovered newspaper serials and short stories)

Titles by Francis Durbridge to be published by Williams & Whiting

A Case For Paul Temple
A Game of Murder
A Man Called Harry Brent
A Time of Day
Bat Out of Hell
Breakaway – The Family Affair
Breakaway – The Local Affair
Death Comes to the Hibiscus (stage play – writing as Nicholas Vane)
La Boutique
Melissa
Murder In The Media
My Friend Charles
Paul Temple and the Alex Affair
Paul Temple and the Canterbury Case (film script)
Paul Temple and the Conrad Case
Paul Temple and the Geneva Mystery
Paul Temple and the Gilbert Case
Paul Temple and the Gregory Affair
Paul Temple and the Jonathan Mystery
Paul Temple and the Lawrence Affair

Paul Temple and the Madison Mystery
Paul Temple and the Margo Mystery
Paul Temple and the Spencer Affair
Paul Temple and the Sullivan Mystery
Paul Temple and the Vandyke Affair
Paul Temple and Steve
Paul Temple Intervenes
Portrait of Alison
Send for Paul Temple (stage play)
Step In The Dark
The Desperate People
The Doll
The Other Man
The Teckman Biography
The World of Tim Frazer
Three Plays for Radio Volume 2
Tim Frazer and the Salinger Affair
Tim Frazer and the Mellin Forrest Mystery
Twenty Minutes From Rome
Two Paul Temple Plays for Radio
Two Paul Temple Plays for Television

Also published by Williams & Whiting:

Francis Durbridge : The Complete Guide
By Melvyn Barnes

This book reproduces Francis Durbridge's original script together with the list of characters and actors of the BBC programme on the dates mentioned, but the eventual broadcast might have edited Durbridge's script in respect of scenes, dialogue and character names.

INTRODUCTION

Francis Durbridge (1912-98) was a prolific writer of sketches, stories and plays for BBC radio from 1933. They were mostly light entertainments, including libretti for musical comedies, but his talent for crime fiction was evident in his early radio plays *Promotion* (1934), *Murder in the Midlands* (1934), *Murder in the Embassy* (1937) and *Information Received* (1938).

The *Radio Times* (11 February 1938) mentioned that Durbridge had by then written some one hundred radio pieces, and Charles Hatton commented in *Radio Pictorial* (28 October 1938) that "He is one of the very few people in this country who have succeeded in making a living by writing for the BBC." Indeed Durbridge continued to provide plays and serials for BBC radio for many years, using his own name and the pseudonyms Frank Cromwell, Nicholas Vane and Lewis Middleton Harvey, while capitalising on a brainwave that defined his name for thirty years.

In 1938 Durbridge had the idea of creating a radio detective called Mark Conway, but soon changed his mind and hit on the dream team of novelist/detective Paul Temple and his wife Steve. His serial *Send for Paul Temple* was a great success, and led to Temple cases over several decades that built an enormous UK and European fanbase. On BBC radio throughout the second half of the twentieth century, Durbridge vied in popularity with fellow thriller writers Edward J. Mason, Lester Powell, Ernest Dudley, Alan Stranks and Philip Levene, but always a new Paul Temple radio serial was a significant event.

Send for Paul Temple was first broadcast from 8 April to 27 May 1938, in eight twenty-five minute episodes. The *Radio Times* maintained an element of mystery by not publishing the actors' names when this serial was broadcast, but simply listed the characters. When the names were eventually released, it was revealed that Hugh Morton and Bernadette Hodgson were the first Paul Temple and Steve. Hugh Morton was to reprise his role in the following two Paul Temple serials, *Paul Temple and the Front Page Men* (1938) and *News of Paul Temple* (1939). Bernadette Hodgson again joined him in these two, but also played Steve in the next serial *Paul Temple Intervenes* (1942) opposite Carl Bernard.

To complete the picture of these early broadcasts, on 13 October 1941 a new production of the original *Send for Paul Temple*, abridged to just one hour, featured Carl Bernard as Temple and Thea Holme as Steve. It also had Cecil Trouncer as Sir Graham Forbes of Scotland Yard – which was unusual, as in this role the actor Lester Mudditt appeared from the initial *Send for Paul Temple* in 1938 and on nineteen occasions until the final episode of *Paul Temple and the Spencer Affair* in 1958. That must surely be some sort of record.

Send for Paul Temple was novelised (John Long, June 1938), written jointly with John Thewes, and much later this provided the basis of another novel *Beware of Johnny Washington* (John Long, April 1951). European translations of *Send for Paul Temple* appeared in France as *La Bande des oiseaux noirs* and in the Netherlands as *Paul Vlaanderen en de ruitenboer*, and its unaccountable absence in Germany has recently been rectified as *Paul Temple und der Fall Max Lorraine*. In the UK, audiobooks were marketed in five cassettes read by Alistair McGowan (ISIS Audiobooks, 1994) and in two CDs (abridged reading by Anthony Head, BBC Audio, 2007.)

The 1938 radio serial *Send for Paul Temple* was so popular that it spawned a theatre play in 1943 (staged in Birmingham and Wolverhampton) and a cinema film in 1946. That film, *Send for Paul Temple* (Butchers/Nettlefold, 1946), with a screenplay by John Argyle and Durbridge, was released in the USA as *Mystery of the Green Finger* and *The Green Finger*; in Germany as *Der Grüne Finger*; in Austria as *Die Todesfalle*; in France as *L'Auberge des tueurs*; and in Denmark as *Den grønne finger*. More significantly, however, it was followed in the UK by the films *Calling Paul Temple* (1948), *Paul Temple's Triumph* (1950) and *Paul Temple Returns* (1952), all of which were based on Durbridge radio serials. And these films were all marketed as the DVD set *The Paul Temple Collection Limited Edition*, Renown Pictures, 2011.

But returning to the original radio production of *Send for Paul Temple*, although no recording has survived there is better news of the Canadian radio production (produced by Andrew Allen for the CBC Dominion Network from 31 May to 19 July 1940). This featured Bernard Braden as Temple and Peggy Hassard as Steve, and interestingly both actors later worked for the BBC and appeared in Durbridge radio serials – Braden as Johnny Washington in 1949 and Hassard in *Paul Temple and the Gilbert Case* in 1954 and the second production of *Paul Temple and the Madison Mystery* in 1955. So the good news is that this Canadian broadcast has survived, and was issued as a CD set by the BBC in 2015; it is also included in the CD set marketed as *Paul Temple : The Complete Radio Collection: The Early Years 1938-1950*, BBC, 2016. The even better news is that the Canadian production, as it followed the original UK script, has enabled this Durbridge script to be transcribed. But to complete the international picture, there was a Dutch radio version - *Spreek met Vlaanderen en het komt in orde*, 12 February to 2 April 1939 in eight episodes, translated by J.C. van der Horst and produced by Kommer Kleijn.

So we can now enjoy this first appearance of the iconic radio detective Paul Temple, with perhaps the signature tune as an earworm - that menacing extract from Rimsky-Korsakov's *Scheherazade* suite, which was used for every Temple serial until giving way in December 1947 to *Coronation Scot* by Vivian Ellis for *Paul Temple and the Sullivan Mystery* and every serial thereafter.

Melvyn Barnes
Author of Francis Durbridge: The Complete Guide (Williams & Whiting, 2018)

SEND FOR PAUL TEMPLE

A radio serial in eight parts

By FRANCIS DURBRIDGE

Broadcast on BBC Radio 8 April – 27 May 1938

Produced by Martyn C. Webster

CAST:

Paul Temple . . . . Hugh Morton

Steve Trent . . . . Bernadette Hodgson

Sir Graham Forbes . . . . Lester Mudditt

Dr Milton . . . . E. Stuart Vinden

Diana Thornley . . . . Cecily Gay

Miss Parchment . . . . Courtney Hope

Pryce . . . . William Hughes

Chief Inspector Dale . . . . Vincent Curran

Horace Daley . . . . Denis Folwell

Inspector Merritt . . . . Cedric Johnson

Dixie . . . . Butts Marchant

Mrs Neddy . . . . Mabel France

Skid Tyler . . . . Hal Bryant

Snow Williams . . . . Wortley Allen

Superintendent Harvey . . . . Duncan Blythe

Alec Rice . . . . John Morley

Episode One

The Green Finger

Announcements. Music.
Fade Music.

SERGEANT: (*On telephone*) Hello? … Hello? … Yes, yes. Who is that? … Oh, hold on a second.

SIR GRAHAM: Well?

SERGEANT: It's Lord Halpick, sir.

SIR GRAHAM: Oh, confound the fellow! This is the second time this morning. All right, give me the phone.

SERGEANT: Very good, sir.

SIR GRAHAM: Wait outside, Sergeant.

SERGEANT: Yes, sir.

SIR GRAHAM: (*On telephone*) Hello? Lord Halpick? This is Sir Graham … Ha? … Oh, no, no, I'm afraid we haven't. Chief Inspector Dale and Chief Inspector Harvey haven't returned from Birmingham yet … Yes, yes, of course … Oh, by all means, Lord Halpick, by all means.

Telephone receiver is replaced.

SIR GRAHAM: Confounded insurance people! I don't know what the devil he thinks we're here for.

A buzzer sounds.

SERGEANT: Inspector Dale and Inspector Harvey, sir.

SIR GRAHAM: Oh good. All right, sergeant, let me have the map I asked for some time before noon.

SERGEANT: Yes, sir.

A door opens.

SIR GRAHAM: Come in, Dale. Come in, Harvey.

Door closes.

HARVEY: Good morning, Sir Graham.

SIR GRAHAM:	Well?
DALE:	It's the same gang, no question of it. Eight thousand pounds worth of diamonds. The nightwatchman is … dead, sir.
SIR GRAHAM:	Dead?
DALE:	Yes. The poor fellow was chloroformed. I don't think they meant to kill him. According to the doctor he was gassed during the war and his lungs were pretty groggy.
SIR GRAHAM:	This is bad, Dale, bad!
DALE:	He was a new man. He'd only been with Stirling's for a month or so.
SIR GRAHAM:	Did you check up on him?
DALE:	Yes. His name was Rogers. Matthew Rogers. Working at Stirling's under the name of Dixon.
SIR GRAHAM:	Had he a record?
HARVEY:	He had a record all right. Everything from petty larceny to blackmail.
DALE:	Inspector Merritt was already on the job when we arrived, sir.
SIR GRAHAM:	Inspector Merritt? (*A pause*) Oh, yes. Who discovered the robbery in the first place?
HARVEY:	One of the constables on night duty, a man called Finlay. He noticed the side door had been forced open – at least that's his story.
SIR GRAHAM:	You don't believe him?
HARVEY:	No. I think he was in the habit of having a chat with Rogers, or Dixon, whichever you like to call him. In fact, he almost admitted as much. He used to make coffee

4

	and I rather think PC Finlay has … a liking for coffee.
SIR GRAHAM:	You think he knew Dixon was an ex-convict?
HARVEY:	No, I don't think so.
SIR GRAHAM:	This is the fourth robbery in two months, Dale. We've got to get them this time! We've got to get them!
DALE:	There wasn't a mark on the safe. If it wasn't for the other robberies, I'd have sworn this was an outside job.
SIR GRAHAM:	What did Merritt have to say?
DALE:	He's in a complete daze, poor devil. He's got some fancy theory about a huge criminal organisation. I think Inspector Merritt has a rather theatrical imagination.
SIR GRAHAM:	You don't think we're up against a criminal organisation then?
DALE:	Well, good Heaven's no. Criminal organisations are all very well between the pages of a novel, sir, but when it comes to real life … well, they just don't exist.
SIR GRAHAM:	Is that your opinion too, Harvey?
HARVEY:	Well, to be perfectly honest, Sir Graham, I'm rather inclined to agree with Merritt. At first I thought we were up against the usual crowd who were having an uncanny run of good luck … but now I'm rather inclined to think otherwise. You see, in the first place there are certain aspects of this business which, to my way of thinking, indicate the existence of a really super mind. A man with an unusual flare for criminal organisation. I know it sounds

	fantastic and all that, sir, I feel rather reluctant to think it myself – but we must face the facts. The facts are pretty grim.
SIR GRAHAM:	Yes.
HARVEY:	First there was the case of Smithson's of Gloucester. Seventeen thousands pounds of stuff spirited away without so much as a by your leave. Then there was the Leicester business. Nine thousand pounds worth. Then there was the Derby affair – four thousand pounds and Mark and me had the Derbyshire area covered. We were in fact, to all intents and purposes, prepared for the raid. But that didn't stop it from happening. Then on top of everything else there's this affair in Birmingham. Eight thousand pounds worth of diamonds. No, Sir Graham, if we were up against the usual crowd – Benny Lever, Dopey Grubbins, Billy Stetson – and all that lot we'd have had them under lock and key ages ago. I firmly believe, Sir Graham, that we're up against one of the greatest criminal organisations in Europe.
SIR GRAHAM:	Yes. (*Pause*) Where was the night watchman when this fellow Finlay discovered him?
HARVEY:	In his usual spot, sir. He had a tiny office in the back of the shop.
SIR GRAHAM:	I suppose you've questioned this man Finlay?
DALE:	Good Lord, yes, sir. I was with him for almost an hour.

SIR GRAHAM:	Did you see the night watchman, Dale, before he died?
DALE:	No, sir, but Harvey did.
SIR GRAHAM:	Well, Harvey?
HARVEY:	He was very groggy when I saw him. The doctor wouldn't let me stay above a couple of minutes.
SIR GRAHAM:	Did he say anything?
HARVEY:	Yes. (*Pause*) Yes, as a matter of fact he did.
SIR GRAHAM:	Well? What did he say?
HARVEY:	Just as I was on the verge of leaving, he turned over on his side and mumbled a few words. They sounded almost incoherent at the time. As a matter of fact, it wasn't until a moment or so later that I realised what he'd said.
SIR GRAHAM:	Well? What did he say?
HARVEY:	He said … "The green finger".
DALE:	The green finger?
HARVEY:	Yes.
DALE:	But that doesn't make sense.
SIR GRAHAM:	Ah, just a minute, Dale, you remember that man we fished out of the river about a month ago. We thought he might have something to do with that job at Leicester. I think you found his print on the back of …
DALE:	(*Interrupting*) Oh yes, Sniper Jackson. I was with Lawrence at the time that he found him. Poor devil was floating down the river like an empty sack. (*A sudden thought*) I say, don't you remember – don't you remember what he said just

7

	before he died? I'm sure I'm right! Why, I believe he said …
SIR GRAHAM:	(*Interrupting*) He said "The green finger!"
DALE:	Yes. "The green finger".
HARVEY:	The same as the night watchman. But what is this "green finger"? What does it mean?
SIR GRAHAM:	That, my dear Chief Inspector Harvey, is one of the many things we are here to find out.
DALE:	I don't think there's any doubt that Sniper Jackson was tied up with that Leicester job. Henderson found two of his fingerprints on one of the showcases.
SIR GRAHAM:	Yes. I reckon that was the reason you and Mullins had the pleasure of … fishing him out of the Thames. The people we're up against know how to deal with incompetence – that's one thing I'll say for them.
DALE:	Sir Graham, do you believe the same as Merritt and Inspector Harvey that we are up against a definite criminal organisation?
SIR GRAHAM:	Yes. Yes, I do, Dale.
DALE:	I suppose you've seen the newspapers, Sir Graham?
SIR GRAHAM:	Oh, yes, yes, yes, I've seen them. Hr'mp! "Send For Paul Temple!" "Why doesn't Scotland Yard send for Paul Temple?" They've even had placards out about the fellow. The press have been very irritating over this affair – very irritating!

DALE:	Paul Temple? Isn't he the novelist chap who helped us over the Tenworthy murder?
SIR GRAHAM:	(*Begrudgingly*) Yes.
DALE:	Well, he caught old Tenworthy, I'll say that for him. By the way, he's a friend of yours, isn't he, Harvey?
HARVEY:	I know him … yes.
SIR GRAHAM:	Temple is just an ordinary amateur criminologist. He had a great deal of luck over the Tenworthy affair. And a great deal of publicity for his novels.
HARVEY:	I don't think Paul Temple exactly courted publicity, Sir Graham.
SIR GRAHAM:	Oh, don't be a fool, Harvey, of course he did! All these amateurs thrive on publicity!
DALE:	Well, you must agree, Sir Graham, we were a little relieved to see the last of the elusive Mr Tenworthy.
SIR GRAHAM:	Yes, and just at the moment, I should be considerably relieved to hear the last of Mr Paul Temple! Ever since this confounded business started people have been bombarding us with letters. "Send for Paul Temple!" "Send for Paul Temple!" "Send –" Well, what is it, Sergeant?
SERGEANT:	The map, sir. You remember you asked me about it?
SIR GRAHAM:	Oh, yes, yes. Well, put it on the desk.
SERGEANT:	Very good, sir.
SIR GRAHAM:	And now, gentlemen (*Opening the map*) You see this map. It's an exact map of the area where so far the criminals have

confined their activities. You'll see the towns that have already been affected – Gloucester, Leicester, Derby and Birmingham. The map's as north as Nottingham and comes as far south as Gloucester – covering, in fact, the entire Midlands. Gentlemen! Somewhere in that area are the headquarters of the greatest criminal organisation in Europe! That organisation must be smashed!

Fade in the sound of people laughing.

DR MILTON: So what did you say?

PAUL TEMPLE: I said, "Dear Madam, the story may be hackneyed, the psychology may be warped, the characters may be unpleasant, but by Timothy the spelling's terrific."

Group laughter.

DIANA: Well, I enjoyed your last book, Mr Temple – even though I didn't guess who committed the murder.

DR MILTON: When did you first start taking an interest in criminology? I mean – an active interest.

PAUL TEMPLE: About two years ago I assisted the police in the investigation of a crime known as the Tenworthy Affair. I had certain theories about the matter which I was able to put into practice. Fortunately, or unfortunately, whichever way one looks at it – they proved successful.

DR MILTON: Tenworthy? Tenworthy? Now, let me see, wasn't that something to do with …

PAUL TEMPLE: (*Interrupting*) It was a murder case, doctor. A man called Tenworthy murdered his wife by gently pushing her over leaning cliffs in Cornwall.

DIANA: How horrible!

PAUL TEMPLE: Yes, it wasn't very pleasant. Naturally, I received a great deal of publicity over the affair and the police, I regret to say, were made to look rather foolish.

DIANA: But you must have taken an interest in the case from the very beginning. I mean, you didn't just sort of … sort of trot along and make a Charlie Chan of the lot of them.

Group chuckling.

DR MILTON: Don't be silly, Diana, Mr Temple is far too modest. I remember reading about the Tenworthy affair. As a matter of fact, they arrested a young fellow called Roberts, who had nothing whatsoever to do with the case, if I remember rightly.

PAUL TEMPLE: Yes, Len Roberts. By Timothy that boy had a near shave.

DIANA: Well, no wonder all the newspapers are saying "Send for Paul Temple".

PAUL TEMPLE: (*Laughs*) The newspapers – like your uncle – are inclined to exaggerate my ability, Miss Thornley. I'm afraid they see in me what is technically described as "good copy".

DIANA: I know the sort of thing. "Popular novelist solves murder mystery!" "Popular novelist defies Scotland Yard!"

PAUL TEMPLE: (*Reticently*) Yes.

11

DR MILTON: I've been reading a great deal about these robberies. They really are remarkable, you know! Four robberies and all within six months. I'm not one for grumbling, but I really do think it's time the police started to show some results. Now look at that business in Birmingham – only this week. According to the papers – nothing's happened about it. The police haven't even got a single clue.

DIANA: Yes, the night watchman was murdered, too.

DR MILTON: Murdered? Oh, I didn't know that.

PAUL TEMPLE: Apparently, he was chloroformed and didn't recover from it. I have a sort of feeling it was an accident.

DR MILTON: Yes … perhaps you're right. (*Pause*) We shall soon start thinking we've settled down in the wrong country, Diana.

Group chuckle.

PAUL TEMPLE: By Timothy, yes!

DR MILTON: It really isn't. I had a drive over to Windrush – it was simply glorious.

DIANA: Mr Temple …

PAUL TEMPLE: Yes?

DIANA: What do you really think about these robberies? Do you think it's the work of an organised sort of – sort of gang – or, or do you think …

DR MILTON: (*Chuckling; interrupting*) Oh, come, Diana, don't start troubling Mr Temple with a lot of newspaper nonsense …

PAUL chuckles.

12

DIANA: No, seriously, I should really like to know what you think about it all.

PAUL TEMPLE: Well, Miss Thornley, if I was Scotland Yard …

DIANA: Yes?

PAUL TEMPLE: If I was Scotland Yard … I should send for Paul Temple.

They all laugh loudly.

Door opens.

PAUL TEMPLE: Yes, Pryce?

PRYCE: Chief Inspector Harvey of Scotland Yard would like to see you, sir.

PAUL TEMPLE: (*A pause; deep in thought*) Chief Inspector Harvey? All right, Pryce, show him in.

Door closes then moments later opens again.

HARVEY: Hello, old boy. Nice to see you again.

PAUL TEMPLE: (*Cheerfully*) Hello, Harvey, how are you?

HARVEY: I'm fine. Believe it or not I'm actually giving crime a rest for a couple of weeks.

PAUL chuckles.

HARVEY: I just happened to be in this part of the world, and I thought I'd drop in on you.

PAUL TEMPLE: Splendid, by Jove, splendid! Harvey, this is a neighbour of mine – Dr Milton, and his niece, Miss Thornley – Chief Inspector Harvey.

HARVEY: How do you do, Miss Thornley? How do you do, doctor?

DR MILTON: How do you do, Inspector? I'm so glad to hear that this isn't a professional visit.

Group chuckle.

DIANA: Don't you think we'd better be making tracks for home, Uncle?

PAUL TEMPLE: Oh, please …

DR MILTON:	No, really, Mr Temple, Diana's right. I never like to be later than ten-thirty if I can possibly help it – and it'll take us at least a quarter of an hour.
PAUL TEMPLE:	Very well, doctor, but don't let the Inspector frighten you away.
DIANA:	(*Chuckling*) It does rather look like a guilty conscience, doesn't it?

They all laugh.

DR MILTON:	Good night, Inspector. I'm glad to have met you.
DIANA:	Good night.
HARVEY:	Good night. Good night, doctor.
PAUL TEMPLE:	I shan't be a second, Harvey, help yourself to a drink.

A door opens.
Harvey pours a drink.
A pause.

PAUL TEMPLE:	Well, Harvey, how are all the bright little boys at Scotland Yard?
HARVEY:	Oh, not very bright, I'm afraid. I say – who did you say that fellow was?
PAUL TEMPLE:	Which fellow? Oh, Dr Milton! He's a retired medico. He bought Ashdown House a couple of months ago. You probably remember the place – used to belong to Lord Snaresdon.
HARVEY:	I thought I'd seen him before somewhere.
PAUL TEMPLE:	You've probably seen his photograph. He's only been in this country since last September. He was a specialist in Sydney, I believe, or somewhere like that. Cigar?
HARVEY:	Thank you.

A pause.

14

PAUL TEMPLE: Well, what brings Chief Inspector Harvey to Bramley Lodge? You don't expect me to swallow that holiday story you handed out?

HARVEY: It did sound rather thin, didn't it?

PAUL TEMPLE: H'm.

HARVEY: Well, I don't suppose you need three guesses to know why I'm here.

PAUL TEMPLE: (*Seriously*) No, I don't, Harvey.

HARVEY: I don't mind telling you – things are in a pretty serious condition at the Yard. In the last six months nearly fifty thousand pounds worth of diamonds have been spirited away from under our very noses. You can take it from me, Temple, this is only the beginning. There'll be bigger stuff than this unless I'm very much mistaken.

PAUL TEMPLE: Go on.

HARVEY: We're up against something we've never even experienced before in this country. A cleverly planned, well-directed, criminal organisation.

PAUL laughs.

HARVEY: I know it sounds fantastic. I know just what you're thinking. But it's the truth, Temple, you can take it from me – it's the truth!

PAUL TEMPLE: Have you made any attempt to trace any of this stuff?

HARVEY: Good heavens, old boy, yes! There isn't a fence in the country we haven't swooped down on.

PAUL TEMPLE: And you haven't found anything?

HARVEY:	Nothing.
PAUL TEMPLE:	Mm. They must be getting the stuff out of the country by some means or other …
HARVEY:	Yes, but how? Not through the usual channels, that we do know.
PAUL TEMPLE:	Who's on this case? Anybody else besides yourself?
HARVEY:	Yes … Dale and a fellow called Merritt. I think you've met him – he's a local.
PAUL TEMPLE:	Yes, I know Inspector Merritt all right. Does Sir Graham know that you've … come to see me?
HARVEY:	Well … as a matter of fact, old man – no! I thought with you being in the actual district we might … sort of …
PAUL TEMPLE:	… Sort of have an unofficial chat about the matter, is that it?
HARVEY:	(*With relief*) Yes. I'm sorry, Temple, but you know what Sir Graham feels about outsiders.
PAUL TEMPLE:	Yes, I know, Harvey. Tell me, Harvey, did you see the night watchman on the Birmingham job? The fellow who died?
HARVEY:	Yes, his name was Rogers. He was an ex-con.
PAUL TEMPLE:	Did he say anything before he …
HARVEY:	(*Interrupting*) I only saw him for a few seconds. The doctor wouldn't let me stay any longer. Whilst I was there, he said, very quietly, "The green finger". At the time I thought the poor fellow was delirious and talking nonsense. Now, however, I'm not so sure…
PAUL TEMPLE:	What makes you say that?

HARVEY:	Well, about a month ago, Dale fished a man out of the Thames. A fellow called Snipey Jackson. He was wanted in connected with the Leicester job. The poor devil was practically gone when we dragged him onto the boat. But Dale is absolutely certain ... he said exactly the same words as the night watchman.
PAUL TEMPLE:	The green finger?
HARVEY:	Yes.
PAUL TEMPLE:	H'm h'm. (*A pause*) When did you come down from London, Harvey?
HARVEY:	This afternoon. I'm staying at the Little General.
PAUL TEMPLE:	The Little General? Oh, you mean the inn! Good Heavens, don't be silly, you must stay here. There's bags of room. We'll run down and get your things.
HARVEY:	Now look here, old boy, I don't want to put you to any trouble.
PAUL TEMPLE:	By Timothy, you're the limit! I'll tell Pryce to get the car ready.

A screech of brakes.

HARVEY:	Coming in?
PAUL TEMPLE:	No, I'll wait outside.
HARVEY:	I shan't be above a minute or two – my things are upstairs.
PAUL TEMPLE:	Yes. Righto.

The sound of a car door closing.

BEN:	Hello, Mr Temple!
PAUL TEMPLE:	Eh?
BEN:	What be'em you doing here at this time of night?

PAUL TEMPLE:	Hello, Ben, I'm just waiting for a friend of mine. How's the farm, eh?
BEN:	Don't talk to me 'o farms. They be more darn trouble than they're worth!
PAUL TEMPLE:	(*Laughing*) Well, here's a cigar, Ben. Have a smoke when you get home.
BEN:	Why, all right, thank you, I will! Make the home smell proper Christmassy this will.
PAUL TEMPLE:	(*Laughs*) Good night, Ben.
BEN:	Good night to y'ee.

Incidental music plays and the sound of crickets.
Suddenly the sound of a man's voice screaming out is heard.
More music.

DALEY:	I say, mister, is that feller a friend of yours? That chap that just come into the inn?
PAUL TEMPLE:	Yes, what's happened?
DALEY:	My God, it's awful! It's awful!
PAUL TEMPLE:	What's happened?
DALEY:	He's shot himself!
PAUL TEMPLE:	(*Pause*) Shot himself? (*After a moment*) No! No, no, that can't be true.
DALEY:	I tell you he's shot himself. I was …
PAUL TEMPLE:	(*Interrupting*) We'd better go inside.

A door opens and the sound of footsteps.
A long silence.

DALEY:	He's dead, in 'e?
PAUL TEMPLE:	Yes. (*Sadly*) He's dead all right.
DALEY:	(*In a panic; upset*) Whatever made him do it? He come in here large as life. What the …
PAUL TEMPLE:	Please. Just a minute.

A long pause.

DALEY:	What are you looking for?
PAUL TEMPLE:	Are you on the telephone?
DALEY:	Yes. It's over there.
PAUL TEMPLE:	(*Quietly*) Thank you.

PAUL lifts the receiver and dials a number.

PAUL TEMPLE:	(*On phone*) Hello? … Sergeant Morrison? … This is Paul Temple speaking … Sergeant, you'd better come along to The Little General … there's been an accident … Well, it might be suicide … Yes, straight away … Oh, and bring Dr Thorne if you can get him … Oh, I see … Well, in that case give Dr Milton a ring and tell him I've been in touch with you … Yes, yes, naturally …

The telephone receiver is replaced.

DALEY:	What did you mean "may be suicide"? You …
PAUL TEMPLE:	(*Angrily interrupting*) What were you doing when my friend arrived?
DALEY:	What was I doing? I – I was doing a crossword puzzle.
PAUL TEMPLE:	Where were you? Behind the bar?
DALEY:	Yes.
PAUL TEMPLE:	Would you mind telling me exactly what happened?
DALEY:	No. No. Of course not. This feller comes in and says he's changed his mind about staying here the night and pops upstairs and brings his suitcase down … there it is, over there.
PAUL TEMPLE:	And then what?
DALEY:	Then he – he asked me if I could change a quid. I says "yes" and goes into the back

19

parlour to get the money. When I gets back, I sees him just as he is now. Laying all twisted up, like, with a gun in his hand. Strewth – I didn't half turn queer.

PAUL TEMPLE: Was anyone else here when he arrived?

DALEY: No, course not. Place has been deserted since half past eight.

PAUL TEMPLE: H'm. (*Pause*) Are you the landlord?

DALEY: Yes, that's me. Horace Daley's the name.

PAUL TEMPLE: You're new here, aren't you?

DALEY: Well, I've been here about six months. I bought the place from a chap called Sharpe. Blimey – he was sharp all right! This place is a proper white elephant.

PAUL TEMPLE: Tell me, could anyone else have come in here whilst you were in the parlour?

DALEY: Not unless they come in from outside or come from upstairs.

PAUL TEMPLE: No one entered from the street – I'm sure of that.

DALEY: I say – why didn't I hear the shot? That's what I can't understand.

PAUL TEMPLE: The gun was fitted with a silencer.

DALEY: Cor – he did himself in in-style, didn't he?

PAUL TEMPLE: (*Surprised*) Hello! He must have been left-handed.

DALEY: Yes. Looks like it, dunn'it? Gun in his left hand all right.

PAUL TEMPLE: Is there any one else staying here at the moment?

DALEY: Yes, an old dame what calls herself Miss Parchment. She arrived yesterday afternoon. Says she's on a walking tour of

20

	the Vale of Evesham. Don't look much like a hiker to me though.
PAUL TEMPLE:	Have you seen her tonight?
DALEY:	Yes. She popped in here about half-past-nine.
PAUL TEMPLE:	H'm. What about the servants?
DALEY:	There's two maids, that's all. The rest sleep out.
PAUL TEMPLE:	I see.
DALEY:	Cor, looks terrible, don't 'e, ay? This business has made me proper nervy.
PAUL TEMPLE:	I think you'd better fetch Miss Parchment down. I'd like to have a word with her.
DALEY:	Miss Parchment? What do we want her for?
PAUL TEMPLE:	The Sergeant will insist on seeing her, so there's no reason why she shouldn't be brought down right away.
DALEY:	All right. If you say so guv'nor.
PAUL TEMPLE:	And you'd better tell her what's happened. We don't want her fainting or anything like that.
DALEY:	If you ask me she'll pass right out!

A door closes as DALEY goes out.

PAUL whistles a few bars of "Early One Morning" as he looks around the place.

PAUL TEMPLE: The bar.

Sound of a handle being turned.

PAUL TEMPLE: H'm h'm.

Door closes again.

PAUL starts to whistle again.

After a few moments a door opens.

PAUL TEMPLE: Well, you've been quick.

DALEY: Yes.

21

PAUL TEMPLE:	Where's Miss Parchment?
DALEY:	She'll be down in a minute.
PAUL TEMPLE:	Have you told her about …
DALEY:	(*Interrupting*) Yes! Would you believe it she was as cool as a cucumber. Talk about some of us men being hard boiled. Why – oh, here she is.
PAUL TEMPLE:	Miss Parchment?
MISS PARCHMENT:	Yes.
PAUL TEMPLE:	My name's Temple – Paul Temple. I'm most awfully sorry to disturb you at this time of night but circumstances …
MISS PARCHMENT:	(*Interrupting*) Oh, please, don't apologise, Mr Temple. Really, what a dreadful business this is. What a dreadful business.
PAUL TEMPLE:	What time was it when you went to your room. Miss Parchment?
MISS PARCHMENT:	Now, let me see, it would be about ten o'clock. I sat for a short while reading. I prefer to read in bed as a rule, but the book I'm reading at the moment is so very interesting …
PAUL TEMPLE:	(*Interrupting*) Yes, I'm sure it is.
MISS PARCHMENT:	I trust you've sent for the police, Mr Temple? I do feel …
PAUL TEMPLE:	(*Interrupting again*) Yes, the Sergeant is on his way here now.
MISS PARCHMENT:	What a dreadful shock it must have been for you. Personally, I can never understand the mentality of anyone

22

	who commits suicide. It always seems to …
PAUL TEMPLE:	What makes you so certain that this is … suicide?
MISS PARCHMENT:	What makes me so certain? But surely it must be suicide. (*Pause*) Unless, of course, Mr Daley shot him.
DALEY:	Here, none of them insinuations. I couldn't kill anyone, see, not even if I wanted to. Can't stand the sight of blood! Makes me proper queer like.
MISS PARCHMENT:	But there doesn't seem to be much blood, Mr Daley.
DALEY:	There's enough to give me the jitters. And if it comes to that, why wasn't you in bed when I knocked on your door?
MISS PARCHMENT:	Because, my dear, Mr Daley, I was reading.
DALEY:	Like to bet it was a murder story.
MISS PARCHMENT:	You'd lose your bet, Mr Daley. It was a book on old English Inns. I'm very interested in old English Inns.
DALEY:	Seems a funny thing to be interested in, to me.
MISS PARCHMENT:	I can assure you – it's most engrossing!
PAUL TEMPLE:	Erm – how long did you intend to stay here, Miss Parchment?
MISS PARCHMENT:	I hadn't quite made up my mind. Most probably till the end of the week.

DALEY:	You didn't say that when you signed the register. You said it was only for one night!
MISS PARCHMENT:	It was my original intention only to stay for the one night – but I've found this Inn so very, very interesting.
DALEY:	Interesting? What the hell's interesting about it?
MISS PARCHMENT:	Why, so many things, my dear Mr Daley. Do you realise the actual Inn itself is over five hundred years old? Think of it – five hundred years!
DALEY:	Well, I've only been here the last six months, and that's long enough for me. The bleeding place is dead after half-past-eight.
PAUL TEMPLE:	Five hundred years? By Timothy, that's certainly a long time. But I was under the impression it was built about seventeen hundred and fifty.
MISS PARCHMENT:	Oh no! Oh, dear, no! It goes back much farther than that.
PAUL TEMPLE:	Then why should it be called The Little General? Surely …
MISS PARCHMENT:	(*Interrupting*) It was re-named The Little General about eighteen hundred and five. Before that it had a much more interesting name.
DALEY:	You seem to know the Dickens of a lot about this place.
MISS PARCHMENT:	It's all in the book I'm reading, Mr Daley. It's all in the book.
DALEY:	Guv'nor, can't we cover him up or somefing till the Sergeant arrives? He

	looks horrible just laying there … staring up at the ceiling.
PAUL TEMPLE:	Yes, yes, all right.
DALEY:	I'll get a sheet from the linen cupboard. I won't be a minute.

A door opens.

MISS PARCHMENT:	Was he a very great friend of yours, Mr Temple?
PAUL TEMPLE:	Not exactly what one would call a "great friend", he was more a sort of … sort of business acquaintance.
MISS PARCHMENT:	I see. You know, when I first saw him, I had a vague sort of suspicion that I'd seen him somewhere before. Of course, one meets …
PAUL TEMPLE:	(*Interrupting*) His name's Harvey – Chief Inspector Harvey of Scotland Yard.
MISS PARCHMENT:	(*Quietly; slightly surprised*) Scotland Yard? Oh dear. Oh dear.

A pause.

PAUL TEMPLE:	You say this Inn wasn't always called The Little General?
MISS PARCHMENT:	No.
PAUL TEMPLE:	Then … what was it called?
MISS PARCHMENT:	(*Starts to laugh slightly hysterically*) A most intriguing title, Mr Temple. I'm sure you'll like it.
PAUL TEMPLE:	Well …
MISS PARCHMENT:	It was called "The Green Finger".

END OF EPISODE ONE

Episode Two

Room Seven

Announcements. Music.
Fade Music.

DALEY:	He's dead, in 'e?
PAUL TEMPLE:	Yes. (*Sadly*) He's dead all right.
DALEY:	Can't – can't we cover him up or somefing till the Sergeant arrives? He looks horrible just laying there … staring up at the ceiling.
PAUL TEMPLE:	Yes, yes, all right.
DALEY:	I'll get a sheet from the linen cupboard. I won't be a minute.

A door opens.

Fade in tense, anxious incidental music playing in the background of the dialogue.

MISS PARCHMENT:	Was he a very great friend of yours, Mr Temple?
PAUL TEMPLE:	Not exactly what one would call a "great friend", he was more a sort of … sort of business acquaintance.
MISS PARCHMENT:	I see. You know, when I first saw him, I had a vague sort of suspicion that I'd seen him somewhere before. Of course, one meets …
PAUL TEMPLE:	(*Interrupting*) His name's Harvey – Chief Inspector Harvey of Scotland Yard.
MISS PARCHMENT:	(*Quietly; slightly surprised*) Scotland Yard? Oh dear. Oh dear.

The incidental music builds to a crescendo and with a crash of cymbals then continues to play slightly quieter in the background under the dialogue.

PAUL TEMPLE: Miss Parchment, you say this Inn wasn't always called The Little General?

MISS PARCHMENT: No.

PAUL TEMPLE: Then … what was it called?

Incidental music again builds and ends suddenly.

MISS PARCHMENT: (*Starts to laugh slightly hysterically*) A most intriguing title, Mr Temple. I'm sure you'll like it.

PAUL TEMPLE: Well …

MISS PARCHMENT: It was called "The Green Finger".

PAUL TEMPLE: (*Thoughtfully*) The Green Finger. Are you sure of this?

MISS PARCHMENT: Oh, quite sure. It's all in the book I'm reading, Mr Temple – a most interesting book.

Door opens.

DALEY: Here's the sheet, guv'nor. Now we can cover him up a bit. If there's anything I hate the sight of it's a feller that's gorn and …

Voices are heard approaching from outside.

DALEY: Hello, what's that?

PAUL TEMPLE: It sounds to me like the Sergeant and Dr Milton.

The voices get louder as they get nearer.

DALEY: Taking a hell of a long time about it.

PC HODGES: Will you want me to remain out here, Sergeant, or come in with you?

MORRISON: You'd better come with me, Hodges.

PC HODGES: Oh, very good, Sergeant.

Door opens.

MORRISON: Good evening, Mr Temple. Evening, Daley.

DALEY:	Thank Heavens you've come. I was just about to …
DR MILTON:	(*Interrupting; shocked*) It's Inspector Harvey! Good gracious! Why … why … this is …
MORRISON:	If you please, doctor.
DR MILTON:	Oh yes. (*Pause*) Yes. I'm sorry, Sergeant. Could we have another light on, please? I can't see very clearly.
MORRISON:	Hodges, just take a look at the back of this place. I think there's some sort of a courtyard.
PC HODGES:	Very good, Sergeant.
MORRISON:	Well, doctor?
DR MILTON:	He's been dead about a quarter of an hour I should say. He must have died almost instantly.
MORRISON:	M'm … Er … M'm … Now, I'd like a few details if you don't mind. Was the deceased a friend of yours, Mr Temple?
PAUL TEMPLE:	Well, not exactly what one would call a friend, Sergeant. I knew him fairly well. His name is Harvey – Chief Inspector Harvey of Scotland Yard.
MORRISON:	Scotland Yard? (*Taking it in*) I see. Was he staying the night here?
DALEY:	Well, he was, and he wasn't, as you might say, Sergeant.
MORRISON:	Well, was he?
PAUL TEMPLE:	Perhaps it would be better if you allowed me to explain, Sergeant.
MORRISON:	Well?
PAUL TEMPLE:	Inspector Harvey was on holiday. He called in to see me about – about ten

31

fifteen this evening. Dr Milton and his niece had been dining with me and were on the point of leaving. Harvey gave me to understand he was staying the night here at The Little General. Unfortunately, I persuaded the poor devil to change his mind and stay the night with me. We came down here to get his luggage.

MORRISON: What time would that be?

PAUL TEMPLE: Oh, about eleven-fifteen I should say, certainly no later.

MORRISON: Go on.

PAUL TEMPLE: Well, I waited outside for him in my car. After about five minutes or so Mr Daley came running out. He was very excited and obviously upset. He told me that Harvey had shot himself.

MORRISON: M'm. Now let's hear your side of the story, Daley.

DALEY: <u>Mr</u> Daley, if you don't mind.

MORRISON: Very well. Let's hear your side of the story, <u>Mr</u> Daley.

DALEY: Well, I was stood behind the bar doing a crossword when this feller comes in and says he's changed his mind about staying here the night. He pops upstairs and brings down his suitcase. Then he asks me if I could change a quid. I says "Yus" and goes into the back parlour to get the money. When I gets back, I sees him just like he is now. Cor, it wasn't half a nasty shock I can tell ya.

MORRISON: M'm. Had you seen him before?

DALEY:	Of course, I had. I was here when he first arrived.
MORRISON:	What time would that be?
DALEY:	Oh, I don't know … about five p'rhaps.
MORRISON:	Was there anyone else in here tonight? When he returned for his luggage?
DALEY:	(*Sarcastically*) Oh, yus, dozens of people! About fifteen platinum blondes and a couple of film stars. We had a Gala Night, Sergeant, you must join in the fun sometime.
MORRISON:	Don't try and be funny and answer the question.
DALEY:	Anyone here at a quarter-past-eleven? Cor, this perishing place is dead after a quarter-past-eight.
MORRISON:	Is there anyone staying here at the moment?
PAUL TEMPLE:	Yes, Sergeant. This lady … Miss Parchment.
MORRISON:	Oh. Oh, yes. Well, ma'am, can … can you throw any light on this matter?
MISS PARCHMENT:	I'm afraid not, Sergeant, I was in my room reading when Mr Daley arrived with the news that this gentleman had shot himself and Mr Temple wished to see me. Naturally, I was dreadfully upset about the matter and …
DALEY:	(*Interrupting*) You didn't look very upset to me!
MISS PARCHMENT:	I have learnt to control my emotions.

33

MORRISON:	Miss Parchment, how long have you been staying here?
MISS PARCHMENT:	I arrived yesterday afternoon, Sergeant. I'm on a walking tour of the Vale of Evesham. I'm interested in old English Inns. Very old English Inns.
MORRISON:	Yes? ... Yes ... Er, just so. Could I have your full name and permanent address?
MISS PARCHMENT:	Certainly. Amelia Victoria Parchment.
MORRISON:	(*Writing it down in his notebook*) Amelia ... Victoria ... Parchment ...
MISS PARCHMENT:	47B, Brook Street, London.
MORRISON:	(*Still writing; quietly*) 47B ... Brook Street ... London ...
MISS PARCHMENT:	Ah, West Central One.
MORRISON:	WC1. Now, thank you. Now, Mr Daley, could anyone have come in here whilst you were in the back parlour?
DALEY:	Yus. They could have either come from upstairs or from the street.
MORRISON:	What about from the back? There's an open courtyard, isn't there?
DALEY:	Yus, but there's no way of getting into the Inn except through the back parlour and I was in there all the time.
MORRISON:	M'm.

Door opens.

MORRISON:	Well, Hodges?
PC HODGES:	There's nothing in the courtyard, Sergeant. Except a lot of blessed pigeons.

DALEY laughs loudly.

MORRISON: M'm. Mr Temple, I wonder if you'd mind running me back to the Station. I feel I ought to have a word with Inspector Merritt about this.

PAUL TEMPLE: Certainly.

MORRISON: Awfully sorry to keep you hanging about, doctor.

DR MILTON: That's all right, Sergeant. That's all right.

MORRISON: The police doc's down with flu, and Mr Temple suggested I …

DR MILTON: (*Interrupting*) Only too glad to be of service, Sergeant. Think nothing of it.

MORRISON: Thank you, sir. You can go to your room, Miss .... Parchment. I doubt whether the Inspector will want to see you tonight.

MISS PARCHMENT: Oh! Thank you. Good night, Sergeant.

Door opens.

MISS PARCHMENT: Good night.

MORRISON: Good night, ma'am.

Door closes.

DALEY: (*Annoyed*) I say, what the hell's going to happen to this fellow? We can't just leave him here all the time.

MORRISON: I'll attend to that, Daley. Hodges, I think you'd better wait at the front – and don't let anyone enter!

PC HODGES: Very good, Sergeant.

PAUL TEMPLE: We'll be as quick as we can, doctor.

DR MILTON: That's all right.

Door opens and closes.

35

A pause.

DALEY: (*Quietly; conspiratorially*) They've gone.

DR MILTON: Yes.

DALEY: I don't like it. I don't like it!

DR MILTON: Don't be a damn fool. Everything's turned out perfectly.

DALEY: You had any more information about the Leamington job?

DR MILTON: Yes. It came through this morning.

DALEY: Well?

DR MILTON: We meet on Tuesday.

DALEY: Tuesdee? Shoo! Here? Or in your place?

DR MILTON: Here.

A long pause.
Fade in.

PRYCE: … At the Police Station here tonight, Chief Inspector Dale discussed with Mr Paul Temple, the celebrated novelist, the incidents leading up to the tragic suicide of Inspector Harvey of Scotland Yard. (*Clears his throat*) It is believed that shortly before his death Chief Inspector Harvey discussed with Mr Temple the mysterious …

PAUL TEMPLE: (*Interrupting*) Right-oh, Pryce.

PRYCE: Shall I read you what the Daily Page says, sir?

PAUL TEMPLE: No. I think we'll leave that to the imagination. Did anyone call yesterday when I was at the Station with Inspector Dale?

PRYCE:	Several reporters, sir – oh, and a rather elderly lady by the name of Miss Parchment.
PAUL TEMPLE:	(*Intrigued*) Miss Parchment? What the devil does she want?
PRYCE:	The lady didn't leave a message, sir.
PAUL TEMPLE:	H'm.
PRYCE:	I'm rather afraid several of the reporters will be returning this morning, sir, they seem quite determined to have a word with you.
PAUL TEMPLE:	(*Brusquely*) I don't want to see any of them. By Timothy, I must get down to that serial, Pryce, I promised to let Malpas have the first instalment by the end of May.
PRYCE:	There was one reporter who seemed very insistent, sir. She simply wouldn't take no for an answer.
PAUL TEMPLE:	(*Intrigued*) Wouldn't she, Pryce?
PRYCE:	A very pretty girl, too, sir … if I may say so.
PAUL TEMPLE:	By all means … say so, Pryce … A very pretty girl who wouldn't take no for an answer … H'm h'm … Sounds interesting …
PRYCE:	(*Annoyed with himself*) Now what was the young lady's name? I made particular note of it because I thought it sounded rather silly for – Ah! Steve! Steve Trent.
PAUL TEMPLE:	Steve Trent? Well, if Miss Steve Trent calls round again – I'm out, Pryce, I haven't the slightest wish …

The doorbell starts to ring.

PRYCE:	It's the door, sir. Excuse me.
PAUL TEMPLE:	It'll be Inspector Dale. You'd better show him in here.
PRYCE:	Very good, sir.

PAUL starts to whistle to himself the tune of "Early One Morning"

PRYCE:	I'm very sorry, miss, but Mr Temple's out.
STEVE:	You told me that yesterday. I'm not …

We hear PRYCE and STEVE TRENT arguing with each other.

PAUL TEMPLE:	What the devil is all this, Pryce? Pryce, who is it?
PRYCE:	It's the young lady, sir …
PAUL TEMPLE:	(*Annoyed*) Which young lady?
PRYCE:	The … er … the reporter, sir.
PAUL TEMPLE:	Oh! Oh, I see!
STEVE:	(*Innocently*) May I come in?
PAUL TEMPLE:	Erm, yes, I think perhaps you'd better. All right, Pryce, you can go.
PRYCE:	Thank you, sir.

Door closes.

STEVE:	He's very determined, isn't he?
PAUL TEMPLE:	Yes, yes, very. I say, look here, you can't come bursting into people's houses like this.
STEVE:	I'm sorry. But you are Paul Temple, aren't you?
PAUL TEMPLE:	Yes.
STEVE:	I tried to see you yesterday, but your man said you were out.
PAUL TEMPLE:	Well, I – (*Impatiently*) What is it you wanted to see me about?
STEVE:	Do you think Chief Inspector Harvey committed suicide?

PAUL TEMPLE:	My dear Miss Trent, I don't see that it makes a great deal of difference what I think.
STEVE:	Please! … Please answer my question! Do you think Chief Inspector Harvey committed suicide?!!
PAUL TEMPLE:	By Timothy, you are a remarkable young woman. First of all, you insult my …
STEVE:	(*Adamantly*) You haven't answered my question!
PAUL TEMPLE:	No. No, I think he was murdered.
STEVE:	(*With relief*) I knew it! I knew it. I knew they'd get him.
PAUL TEMPLE:	Why do you say that?
STEVE:	Gerald Harvey was … a friend of mine.
PAUL TEMPLE:	Oh! Oh, I'm sorry. My man told me that you were a reporter and …
STEVE:	(*Interrupting*) Yes, that's true. I'm on the staff of the Evening Post – but that's not why I wanted to see you.
PAUL TEMPLE:	Why did you want to see me?
STEVE:	Because I need your help. Because I need your help more than I've ever wanted anything else in my life before.
PAUL TEMPLE:	Was Harvey … a very great friend of yours?
STEVE:	(*Quietly*) He was my brother.
PAUL TEMPLE:	(*Surprised; sympathetically*) Your brother?
STEVE:	Yes. My real name is Harvey – Louise Harvey. I just use the name of Steve Trent partly for professional reasons and … partly for another reason too …

PAUL TEMPLE: When I suggested that your brother might have been murdered you said "I knew it. I knew it. I knew they'd get him". What did you mean by "I knew they'd get him"?

STEVE: Why do you think my brother came to see you, Mr Temple? The night he was murdered.

PAUL TEMPLE: I don't know. I'm not at all certain he had any particular reason.

STEVE: (*Sharply*) He had! A very good reason!

PAUL TEMPLE: Well?

STEVE: My brother was investigating the mysterious robberies that have been occurring. He had a theory about these robberies which I believe he wanted to discuss with you.

PAUL TEMPLE: A theory?

STEVE: About eight years ago my brother was attached to what was then called The Service B.Y. – it was a special branch of the Cape Town Constabulary. At this particular time a very daring, and successful gang of criminals, were carrying out a series of raids on various jewellers within a certain area known as the Cape Town Simons Town area. My brother, and another officer whose name I forget at the moment, were in charge of the case. After months of investigation they discovered that the leader of the organisation was a man who called himself The Knave of Diamonds – but his real name was Max Lorraine. Lorraine, apparently, was a well-educated man who, at one time, had occupied an important position at Columbo University. Eventually, the organisation was smashed. But Lorraine had made his plans very carefully … and he escaped. Two months later, the officer who had assisted my brother in the investigation was murdered. It was not a pleasant murder. This was followed almost immediately by two attempts on my brother's life.

PAUL TEMPLE: (*Gently*) Please, go on.

STEVE: From the very first moment when Gerald was put in charge of this Midlands case, he had an uneasy feeling, at the back of his mind, that he was up against Max Lorraine. I saw him a few days before he came up to see you, and he told me then that he was almost certain that Max Lorraine, alias The Knave of Diamonds, was the real influence behind the robberies which he and Inspector Dale were investigating. I think he was a little worried. Rather frightened.

PAUL TEMPLE: Had your brother discussed with Sir Graham, and any of his colleagues, his theory about this man Lorraine?

STEVE: No – no, I don't think so.

PAUL TEMPLE: Why not?

STEVE: Because he knew only too well that they would never believe him.

PAUL TEMPLE: Never believe him?

STEVE: The Knave is hardly the sort of person one can talk about and … sound convincing. He's like a character snatched from the

41

most sensational thriller … and imbued with a strange satanic intellect. (*Angrily*) You think that sounds silly, don't you?

PAUL TEMPLE: Well, er … it sounds a little unusual …

STEVE: (*Desperately*) Mr Temple, do you believe me? Do you believe my story about this man Lorraine?

PAUL TEMPLE: (*After a moment*) Yes. (*Quietly*) Yes, I do believe you. Tell me, did your brother ever see him? Did they ever meet?

STEVE: No. No, not once. But he knew his methods. He knew everything about him. And he was afraid.

PAUL TEMPLE: The night your brother came to my house, he told me he was firmly convinced that a well-directed criminal organisation existed. But … he didn't mention anything about this man Max Lorraine. Why not, I wonder?

STEVE: I don't know. He intended to, I'm sure of that. He wanted your help over this case. He had a very great admiration for you. It was Gerald who persuaded me to start the "Send For Paul Temple" campaign in the Evening Post.

PAUL TEMPLE: By Timothy, you certainly started something. A little while ago you said you chose the name of Steve Trent not only for professional reasons but partly for another reason too. What did you mean by that?

STEVE: Gerald was terrified that Lorraine might find out that he had a sister. Even in Cape Town, Gerald made me live with relatives under an assumed name.

PAUL TEMPLE:	Was he naturally precautious about everything?
STEVE:	No, but he knew that Max Lorraine would stop at nothing.
PAUL TEMPLE:	Your brother must have known a great deal about this man.
STEVE:	Yes … a great deal. And the day before he died … he passed that information on to me!
PAUL TEMPLE:	To you?!! That may mean danger … great danger. You realise that?
STEVE:	Yes.
PAUL TEMPLE:	What is it you know about Max Lorraine?
STEVE:	I know … that he has a small scar above the right elbow. That he smokes Russian cigarettes. And he's devoted to a girl who answers to the name of Ludmilla.

Deep in thought PAUL starts whistling the same tune again.

PAUL TEMPLE:	Miss Trent, you said you wanted my help. You said you wanted my help more than you wanted anything else in your life before. What did you mean by that?
STEVE:	(*Boldly*) I meant, that from now on, I want it to be Paul Temple versus Max Lorraine!

PAUL laughs.

STEVE:	Well, why are you laughing?
PAUL TEMPLE:	I was just thinking of something Pryce said before you arrived here.
STEVE:	Well?
PAUL TEMPLE:	He said … you simply wouldn't take no for an answer.

Melodramatic incidental music.

DR MILTON: Now that I've shown you, is that quite clear, Dixie?

DIXIE: Yes, it seems quite clear. Diana will be parked at the corner of Regent Street. I've got to get from the jewellers to the car, pass the stuff over, and then mingle with the crowd in front of the dress shop.

DR MILTON: Yes, that's right. And stay there! Don't make any attempt to sneak away until the crowd moves.

DIXIE: Don't worry – I won't.

DR MILTON: Have you looked the place over?

DIXIE: Yes. I had a look round this morning. Yeah, not very difficult. I should be out in a little under seven minutes.

DR MILTON: Good. Now, Skid, I want you to have a look at this map.

Sound of the map being opened.

SKID: Okay, Dr Milton, I'm looking …

DR MILTON: See Regent Street?

SKID: Yeah, I see it.

DR MILTON: That's where Diana will park the car. Now take a look at the corner. You can see the jewellers and the dress shop the moment you come round the bend. The Chief wants you to come round that corner at 7.40 precisely! You should reach the dress shop about 7.41. Then let it rip! Got that?

SKID: Yeah, I got it all right.

DR MILTON: And we want a good job made of this. No half measures. Straight through the dress shop window! You understand, Skid?

SKID: Sure …

DR MILTON: We want noise! And plenty of it!

44

SKID:	Don't worry – I'll wake up the whole blasted town.
DR MILTON:	Good.
DALEY:	Well, thank Gawd it's you on the lorry and not me.
DR MILTON:	Shut up, Horace! You'll be all right, Skid, if you keep your head. All you've got to do is to make it look genuine.
SKID:	It'll look genuine all right.
DR MILTON:	Well, I hope so.
DIXIE:	Do I wait for the smash before I …
DR MILTON:	(*Interrupting*) No! At 7.40 get to work. You won't have much time but it shouldn't take any longer than the Gloucester job.
DIXIE:	Don't worry about me, doc. I'll be out of there in no time. Have you got a list of the stuff?
DR MILTON:	I'm expecting Diana with it. She went to see the Chief this morning.
SKID:	I say, doc, who is this feller calls himself The Knave? He's been running us around now for three months and we ain't even so much had a glimpse of him. Don't you think that we ought to…
DIXIE:	(*Interrupting*) That don't worry me who the feller is – he could be Sir Graham Forbes himself as far as I'm concerned. All I know is … he can certainly organise. A cool forty thousand in three months. Boy! That's what I call money!
SKID:	I'm not a grumbler. I'm just sort of curious, that's all.
DALEY:	Same 'ere. Who the 'ell is The Knave, doc?

DR MILTON: You'll find out, my friends, all in good time. (*Chuckling to himself*) All in good time.

DIXIE: Say, doc, where do you come into this Leamington job? Does Diana …

DR MILTON: (*Interrupting*) As soon as you pass the stuff to Diana she drives straight to Warwick. I take it over at Warwick and get the stuff back here. Horace does the rest. It'll be in Amsterdam by Saturday.

DIXIE: Any idea what cut we're going to get out of this?

DR MILTON: I'm not sure. Frobisher's has got a pretty heavy stock. There's a ring worth six thousand pounds.

SKID: Six thousand?

DALEY: Whow!

DIXIE: The Knave can certainly pick 'em!

There is a single knock on wood.

SKID: Wait a minute!

Two more knocks.

A pause.

One knock.

A pause.

Two more knocks.

SKID: There's somebody at the panel!

Two more knocks.

A pause.

Two more knocks.

DR MILTON: It's all right, Skid, it's only Diana.

DALEY: Blimey! You ain't 'alf jumpy!

The sound of a wooden panel sliding open.

DIANA: Sorry I'm late, Doc. No, don't shut the panel.

DR MILTON: Why not?

DIANA: The Chief's coming.

46

SKID: The Chief!
DIXIE: Blimey!
DR MILTON: Here?
DIANA: Yes.
DR MILTON: Oh. Still, I think we'd better shut it.
The shutter is pushed closed.
SKID: He's coming here? The Knave?
DIANA: Yes, he's got the Birmingham money. It came
             through this morning.
DIXIE: Blimey, that's quick work!
DIANA: Have you given them the Leamington details?
DR MILTON: Yes.
DIANA: How do you feel about it, Skid? Think you can
             manage the smash all right?
SKID: Yes, as easy as falling off a log.
DIANA: Good. We want as much row as possible.
             Remember that. As soon as you hit the dress
             shop you might work it that your horn sticks.
             You ought to be able to fix that all right.
SKID: Sure!
DIANA: And don't forget to dash back to the shop,
             Dixie – there's bound to be a crowd.
DIXIE: Okay. Have you got a list of the stuff?
DIANA: Yes. Here we are.
A pause.
DIXIE: Phew!
SKID: Any good, Dixie?
DIXIE: Any good?
Another single knock.
SKID: Answer that!
Two more knocks.
A pause.
Two more knocks.
DIANA: It's the Chief! Open the panel, Doc.

The panel is pulled open again.

DR MILTON: Gentlemen, meet The Knave!

SKID: The Knave!

DALEY: I thought you said that …

DIXIE: (*Shocked*) What? What? This isn't The Knave!

DR MILTON: Surprised, gentlemen? Surprised? (*Begins to chuckle to himself*)

END OF EPISODE TWO

Episode Three

Murder At Scotland Yard

Announcements. Incidental Music
Fade Music

DR MILTON:	Gentlemen, meet The Knave!
SKID:	The Knave!
DALEY:	I thought you said that …
DIXIE:	(*Shocked*) What? What? This isn't The Knave!

Pause.

Fade In.

PAUL TEMPLE: Would you care for a liqueur, Steve?

STEVE: No. I don't think so, thanks.

PAUL TEMPLE: Nonsense! By Timothy, this coffee needs it. Pryce, a Cherry Brandy for Miss Trent!

PRYCE: Certainly, sir.

PAUL TEMPLE: Well, it was very decent of you to come down from Town at a moment's notice like this. I hope it wasn't too inconvenient.

STEVE: No, of course not, but – but why did you send for me so suddenly?

PAUL TEMPLE: Well, Steve, because … oh, by the way, I've decided to drop the Miss Trent. It reminded me of a rather elderly lady I met at a garden party. She thought I was part author of Gone with the Wind.

Steve laughs loudly and happily.

PRYCE: Cherry Brandy, miss.

STEVE: Oh! Thank you.

Door closes as PRYCE goes out.

PAUL TEMPLE: I sent for you, Steve, because I've been thinking of what you told me the other day.

STEVE:	You mean about my brother … and Max Lorraine.
PAUL TEMPLE:	Yes. If your brother was right and this man Lorraine, alias The Knave, really is the big noise behind these jewel robberies then … I think you should tell Sir Graham all you know about him.
STEVE:	He'd never believe me! This man Lorraine …
PAUL TEMPLE:	(*Interrupting*) I'm not so sure that he wouldn't, Steve. The Chief Commissioner isn't quite such a fool as people think. He's got his head screwed on all right. Even though he won't "Send for Paul Temple".
STEVE:	But they don't even believe my brother was murdered. If they think he committed suicide, then they …
PAUL TEMPLE:	(*Interrupting*) I can prove to them that he didn't commit suicide … if they need any proof.
STEVE:	You can?
PAUL TEMPLE:	Yes. According to Horace Daley, the landlord of The Little General, when your brother came downstairs, he asked him to change a pound note. And Daley then went into the back parlour to get the money.
STEVE:	Well?
PAUL TEMPLE:	Well, why should he go into the back parlour? There was thirty-seven and sixpence in the till which was on the bar counter. It doesn't make sense.
STEVE:	How do you know this?

PAUL TEMPLE:	Because I examined the till when Daley went upstairs to fetch Miss Parchment down. In fact, that's why I sent him.
STEVE:	M'm. Of course, there may be a perfectly simple explanation. Perhaps the landlord only went …
PAUL TEMPLE:	(*Interrupting*) Oh yes! There might be quite a simple explanation. But there's just one other little point … Your brother was holding the revolver in his left hand.
STEVE:	But Gerald was left-handed.
PAUL TEMPLE:	Yes. Of course … That's just the point!
STEVE:	What do you mean?
PAUL TEMPLE:	I mean, my dear Miss Trent, that your brother was murdered by someone with a little too much imagination … and not sufficient intelligence.
STEVE:	But if it's so very obvious that my brother was murdered – why do the police think he committed suicide?
PAUL TEMPLE:	What makes you so certain that the police think he committed suicide?
STEVE:	Why, it's been in all the newspapers … and even at the Inquest they … You think they know he was murdered?
PAUL TEMPLE:	I'm almost sure of it.
STEVE:	Then why on earth did they make it out to be suicide? Surely …
PAUL TEMPLE:	(*Interrupting*) I expect they have a reason, Steve. And I shouldn't be surprised if it wasn't a very good one.
STEVE:	Who was the lady who was staying at the Inn? Miss – er …

PAUL TEMPLE: Miss Parchment? She's a retired school-mistress with a passion for old English Inns. (*Imitating the way Miss Parchment speaks*) "Very old English Inns". Why do you ask?

STEVE: Oh, no particular reason. I noticed her at the Inquest, that's all. I called in at The Little General the last time I was down here. (*Adamantly*) I don't trust that man Daley! There's something about him that makes me suspicious.

PAUL TEMPLE: Yes … Yes, I can understand that. As a matter of fact, there's something rather peculiar about the Inn itself, if you ask me.

STEVE: Why do you say that?

PAUL TEMPLE: Well, according to Miss Parchment, the Inn wasn't always called The Little General. It used to be known as The Green Finger.

STEVE: (*Perplexed*) The Green Finger? That's a peculiar name.

PAUL TEMPLE: Yes, it's peculiar in more senses than one. After the Birmingham robbery the night watchman died. He was chloroformed. Before he died, however, he said, "The Green Finger".

STEVE: You don't think … this Inn – The Little General – is used as a sort of meeting place. That would account for …

PAUL TEMPLE: (*Interrupting*) Yes, I did think of that.

STEVE: It might be a good idea to have the place watched.

PAUL TEMPLE: Merritt's watching it. He'll let me know if anything funny happens.

STEVE: Merritt? Who's Merritt?

PAUL TEMPLE: Don't tell me you've never heard of Inspector Charles Mortimer Merritt. Dear, oh dear, he won't be flattered!

STEVE: Oh, I remember … He was helping Gerald and Chief Inspector Dale over the jewel robberies. Is he a friend of yours?

PAUL TEMPLE: By Timothy, yes! Merritt and I get along like a house on fire! He's a funny little devil … always got some wild sort of theory at the back of his head – but he's really as cute as a box of monkeys. You'd like him.

STEVE: Have you known him long?

PAUL TEMPLE: Mm, about five or six years. He hasn't been in this country all that long. He was out in New Zealand for a little while, I think. Well, somewhere like that. If he wasn't so damn rude to his superiors, they'd have had him at the Yard ages ago.

STEVE: Paul, do you really think I ought to tell Scotland Yard about what Gerald thought about The Knave being responsible …

PAUL TEMPLE: (*Interrupting*) Yes, I do, Steve. Believe me, I'll do all I possibly can to help you, my dear, I promised you that. But until Scotland Yard finally decide …

The telephone starts to ring.

PAUL TEMPLE: Excuse me.

STEVE: Certainly.

The sound of PAUL lifting the telephone receiver.

PAUL TEMPLE: (*On phone*) Hello? … Yes, Paul Temple speaking … Who is that? … Oh, Inspector Dale! … Hello, Dale, how are you? …

Yes, I'm pretty fit, thanks … I beg your pardon? … Yes … Yes … When does he want to see me? … Oh … All right … Tell Sir Graham I'll be there. Thank you for ringing … Goodbye.

PAUL replaces the telephone receiver.

PAUL TEMPLE: That was Dale, of Scotland Yard. He was speaking for the Chief Commissioner.

STEVE: (*Hopefully*) Well?

PAUL TEMPLE: They want to see me.

STEVE: To see you? That can only mean …

PAUL TEMPLE: (*Interrupting*) That can only mean one of two things. They either want to know the reason why your brother visited me the night he was murdered, or they've decided …

STEVE: (*Interrupting; triumphantly*) To "Send for Paul Temple".

PAUL TEMPLE: Yes.

Door opens.

PRYCE: Inspector Merritt, sir!

Long pause.

CONSTABLE: (*With authority*) I'm sorry, miss, but you can't park here!

DIANA: Oh, really, officer, I'm most awfully sorry, I promised to meet a friend here and …

CONSTABLE: (*Interrupting*) I'm sorry, miss, you'll have to take it round to Victoria Square.

DIANA: But couldn't I stay here for just a little while? I know it's most irregular.

CONSTABLE: Well, then, it won't have to be for long, miss.

DIANA:	(*With charm*) No, of course not. It's really most awfully kind of …
CONSTABLE:	(*Interrupting*) Well, that's all right, miss. Sorry to such a nuisance but, you know what it is, we fellows have to keep on the job.
DIANA:	Why, yes, of course.
CONSTABLE:	I was only saying to the Sergeant last Monday, the old parking problem could be settled as easy as pie, if only the local authorities would have the common sense to er …
DIANA:	What's the matter?
CONSTABLE:	Look at that lorry coming down the hill. He's going all over the place! Good God he's going for the pavement! Look out there!

The sound of pedestrians screaming as they see the lorry approaching them at break-neck speed.

The sound of breaking glass as the lorry crashes through the dress shop window.

The sound of a horn continually blaring.

An alarm bell starts ringing.

CONSTABLE:	(*Shouting orders; trying to take control of the situation*) All right, come now, make way there, if you don't mind, sir. Step to one side, madam. Get off the pavement, please! (*Getting angry*) Step to one side, sir! Now, what's all this? Anybody hurt?
SKID:	No, thank heavens. It was the steering, Constable. As I came round the corner, something went wrong and I …

CONSTABLE:	(*Interrupting*) You must stop that alarm. Where the devil is … Hello, what's that bell? That sounds to me like …
SKID:	(*Slightly panicky*) It's the burglar alarm! Them wires must have been across the winders and when I went through …
CONSTABLE:	(*Barking instructions*) Everyone to one side, please! Can't you see …
SKID:	(*Interrupting*) Just a minute, constable, I feel like a bag of nerves!
CONSTABLE:	It's a miracle to me no one was hurt. Well – they must stop that noise! (*Start fade*) Step on one side, please!

Fade the alarms slightly.

DIANA:	(*Urgently*) Have you got the stuff?
DIXIE:	Have I? Thank God, what a smash! It sounded like it was just on top of me! Is Skid all right?
DIANA:	I don't know. Drop the bag in the back! Quick!
DIXIE:	I think I ought to come with you …
DIANA:	(*Interrupting; very insistent*) No! Go back to the dress shop and mix with the crowds. Be quick, Dixie, be quick!
DIXIE:	Okay. Take care of that bag!

The sound of a car engine starting up.
Dramatic incidental music booms in and stops suddenly.

PRYCE:	Inspector Merritt, sir!
PAUL TEMPLE:	Hello, Charles! This is a pleasant surprise.
MERRITT:	I just thought I'd drop in for a chat. I happened to be passing.
PAUL TEMPLE:	Why yes, of course. I don't think you know Miss Trent.

MERRITT:	Inspector Merritt.
STEVE:	How do you do, Inspector?
MERRITT:	How do you do, Miss Trent? I hope I haven't interrupted anything?
PAUL TEMPLE:	(*Chuckling*) Well, of course not, Charles. Have you had dinner?
MERRITT:	Aye. But if there's any of that really excellent brandy of yours …
PAUL TEMPLE:	(*Laughs*) Help yourself, old man. It's on the cocktail cabinet.
MERRITT:	Ah, thanks.
STEVE:	Well, I really think I ought to be getting along, Paul. If you're coming down to Town tomorrow …
PAUL TEMPLE:	(*Interrupting*) I'll pick you up at about three. We'll go along to the Yard together, Steve.
STEVE:	(*Anxiously*) You really think I ought to tell Sir Graham all I know?
PAUL TEMPLE:	Yes … Yes, I do.
STEVE:	(*Quietly*) Very well. Good night, Inspector.
MERRITT:	Good night, Miss Trent.

A door opens.

A pause.

Door closes.

MERRITT:	I say, look here, Paul, I hope I haven't butted in on a private …
PAUL TEMPLE:	(*Interrupting*) No, of course not, Charles, of course not. How's the brandy?
MERRITT:	Fine … She's a pretty girl, isn't she?
PAUL TEMPLE:	Yes. Yes, she is, rather. Surprised you've never met her before. She's a reporter on the Evening Post.

MERRITT:	What did you say her name was? Trent?
PAUL TEMPLE:	Yes. Steve Trent. At least, that's the name she works under on the newspaper. Her real name is Harvey. Louise Harvey. She's the sister to Inspector Harvey. The fellow who was …
MERRITT:	(*Interrupting; shocked*) Sister!
PAUL TEMPLE:	(*Quietly*) Yes. Why? What's the matter?
MERRITT:	Oh … nothing. Only … I never knew Harvey had a sister. Why wasn't she at the inquest?
PAUL TEMPLE:	She was … but she didn't give evidence. (*A pause*) Well! Any news?
MERRITT:	I've had the Inn watched. Everything seems to be above board as far as I can make out.
PAUL TEMPLE:	M'm.
MERRITT:	I've checked up on that Green Finger story. The Inn did used to be known at The Green Finger, but that's certainly going back some years.
PAUL TEMPLE:	I still think there's something funny about that Inn, Charles. I don't know what it is – but I intend to find out.
MERRITT:	Aye, I think there's something there, too.
PAUL TEMPLE:	Oh, by the way, you might be interested to know that the Chief Commissioner wants to see me.
MERRITT:	He does? Well, that's definitely good news.
PAUL TEMPLE:	Of course, he may only want to ask me a few questions about this business with Harvey. On the other hand …

MERRITT:	(*Interrupting*) Oh, just a minute, Paul, I have got a bit of news – I was forgetting. One of my men went into The Little General yesterday morning, and on coming out he bumped into another fellow known as Skid Tyler.
PAUL TEMPLE:	(*Taking this in*) Skid Tyler?
MERRITT:	Aye. Know anything about him?
PAUL TEMPLE:	I don't know. Skid Tyler? Skid … Yes, I've got him! He used to be a driver at Brooklands. He was warned off the track in 1930 and served a term of imprisonment in 1931 for share pushing … or was it 32, I'm not sure which, but …
MERRITT:	(*Interrupting*) Well, that's the fellow, anyway.
PAUL TEMPLE:	I wonder what he was doing at The Little General.
MERRITT:	Aye, that's what I wondered. I sent a man back to trail him … but the idiot bungled the job and Skid disappeared.
PAUL TEMPLE:	Oh. Did you check up on Miss Parchment?
MERRITT:	Aye. She's all right as far as I can make out. Retired school mistress – lives alone in a small flat in Tottenham Court Road. Passionately fond of reading, and old English Inns. Seems a hell of a life to me – but it seems genuine enough.
PAUL TEMPLE:	Somehow, I feel sure that in some peculiar way Miss Parchment fits into all this mystery about The Little General, Harvey's murder and the jewel robberies. I don't know how, but I'm sure she does.

61

MERRITT:	Well, your hunches aren't often wrong, Paul. I fail to see how an innocent old dame with a passion for Eng …

Telephone starts to ring.

PAUL TEMPLE:	(*Interrupting*) Excuse me, a minute.

Telephone continues to ring.

PAUL lifts the receiver.

PAUL TEMPLE:	(*Into phone*) Hello, Paul Temple speaking … Yes … Yes! … It's for you, Charles.
MERRITT:	Oh, thanks. (*Into phone*) Hello! … Who is that? … Oh, hello, Sergeant … Aye … Aye … Aye … Go on! … Good Lord! … Yes, of course. You'd best pick me up here … Yes, good-bye.

The telephone receiver is replaced.

PAUL TEMPLE:	What's happened?
MERRITT:	They've done it again.
PAUL TEMPLE:	You mean …
MERRITT:	(*Interrupting*) It's Leamington, this time. Frobishers of Regent Street. Fourteen thousand pounds worth of stuff.
PAUL TEMPLE:	By Timothy!
MERRITT:	There'll be hell to pay over this!
PAUL TEMPLE:	When did it happen?
MERRITT:	About a quarter of an hour ago. Practically in broad daylight. That smash sounds a damn funny business to me.
PAUL TEMPLE:	(*Urgently*) What smash?
MERRITT:	A lorry crashed into a dress shop which was next door to the jewellers. It were such a devil of a row with the smash that no one took the slightest notice of what was happening next door.
PAUL TEMPLE:	It sounds like a cover to me.

MERRITT: Aye, that's what I thought.

PAUL TEMPLE: Charles! Tell them to hold that lorry driver!

MERRITT: Why?

PAUL TEMPLE: Because by Timothy, I bet a fiver it's Skid Tyler!

Long pause.

Fade up.

SIR GRAHAM: Very interesting. You say that from the very beginning your brother was under the impression that the brains behind these robberies was this man, er – Max Lorraine. The man who calls himself The Knave of Diamonds.

STEVE: Yes.

SIR GRAHAM: H'm. Well, what do you think of all this, Temple?

PAUL TEMPLE: Well, Sir Graham, I don't think there's any doubt that we're up against a definite criminal organisation whose activities are organised by a man who … well, to say the least of it … is out of the ordinary run of criminals.

SIR GRAHAM: Yes, I agree with you there. But that doesn't necessarily mean that we're up against this man Miss Trent talks about – The Knave of Diamonds.

PAUL TEMPLE: No … but, nevertheless, I think we are, Sir Graham. Harvey was no fool. Harvey was convinced in his own mind that we were up against The Knave. (*Pause*) And he was murdered.

63

SIR GRAHAM:	(*Gravely*) What makes you so certain that Harvey was murdered?
PAUL TEMPLE:	Because it's as obvious as daylight. He was holding the revolver in his left hand. And the poor devil had been shot through the back of his left shoulder. Harvey was left-handed all right, but I hardly think he was a contortionist into the bargain.
SIR GRAHAM:	Yes, that's true. (*Pause*) Harvey was murdered. We spotted it immediately. I was surprised the doctor didn't.
PAUL TEMPLE:	But the police doctor was down with flu. A Dr Milton came along with the Sergeant. He's a retired medico who happens to be an acquaintance of mine. Still, I must admit, I did think it was rather funny he never noticed it.
SIR GRAHAM:	It is strange. When was the last time you saw your brother?
STEVE:	The day before he visited Mr Temple.
SIR GRAHAM:	Oh, yes, I see. Did he seem cheerful and … erm … in normal health?
STEVE:	Yes, I think so. We never really saw a great deal of one another, you know, my work kept me busy quite a lot and he was always dashing out of Town on some case or other.
SIR GRAHAM:	Ah, yes, of course.
PAUL TEMPLE:	I saw Merritt last night and he told me about this business at Leamington. Did you hold the driver of the lorry?
SIR GRAHAM:	Yes. You were right about that, by the way. It was Skid Tyler.
PAUL TEMPLE:	Have you questioned him?

SIR GRAHAM:	Not yet. Merritt's bringing him here this afternoon. I've got a feeling that Tyler might talk.
PAUL TEMPLE:	Yes … he might.
SIR GRAHAM:	I don't expect he'll know a great deal. He's most probably one of the small fry. On the other hand – you never can tell.
PAUL TEMPLE:	Sir Graham …
SIR GRAHAM:	Yes?
PAUL TEMPLE:	Why did you send for me this afternoon?
SIR GRAHAM:	(*Clears his throat*) Yes, I … I've been waiting for you to ask that question.
PAUL TEMPLE:	Well?
SIR GRAHAM:	Well, ever since these robberies first started – there's been a definite campaign, both in the newspapers and among a certain section of the public, urging us to, er …
STEVE:	To "Send for Paul Temple"?
SIR GRAHAM:	Yes, Miss Trent. To (*Clears throat again*) send for Paul Temple. Well, I – I don't mind telling you, Temple, the whole damned campaign got me rattled! I was convinced in my own mind that there was nothing you could possibly do to, er … to assist us in this matter. Now, however, I'm not so certain. You see, Temple, and I'm sure I can speak in confidence before Miss Trent, there's certain aspects about this business that are very confusing. And which, instead of getting clearer, tend towards leading us further and further into a confusing mass of … what seems to be on the surface – melodramatic nonsense!

| | But is it nonsense? That's just the point. Now, now take all this business about The Green Finger. We know that the Little General Inn used to be called The Green Finger. We know that the night watchman murmured "The Green Finger" before he died. But what does it mean? What is "The Green Finger"? And then, secondly, there's the matter of district. That's been puzzling me a lot lately. Why should this organisation confine its activities entirely to the Midlands? And then, then there's another point … and believe me, a very important one. How in Heaven's name are they getting the stuff out of the country? And they must be getting the stuff out of the country – because if it was still over here, you can take it from me, Temple, we'd have it back in twenty-four hours. |

PAUL TEMPLE: H'm. Well, Sir Graham, I don't profess to be able to work miracles – by profession, I'm a writer. But, well I must confess, I'm very intrigued by a certain aspect of this affair.

SIR GRAHAM: Well, then, we can count on you to …

PAUL TEMPLE: You can count on me to give you every assistance in my power, Sir Graham. That, I promise you.

SIR GRAHAM: Thank you, Temple. I was hoping you'd say that.

Door opens.

DALE: Oh, I'm sorry, sir, I thought that …

SIR GRAHAM:	(*Interrupting*) Come in, Dale! Come in. You know Paul Temple, I believe. Inspector Dale.
PAUL TEMPLE:	Yes, yes …
DALE:	Of course.
SIR GRAHAM:	And Miss Trent?
DALE:	How do you do?
STEVE:	How do you do, Inspector?
DALE:	I thought perhaps you'd like to know Inspector Merritt has arrived, sir, with that man … er, Tyler – Skid Tyler.
SIR GRAHAM:	Oh, well, er, when I ring – show them in here.
DALE:	Very good, sir.
Door closes.	
SIR GRAHAM:	Would you, er, like to stay while we question this man?
PAUL TEMPLE:	Yes. Yes, I would, rather.
SIR GRAHAM:	Good. I should sit over there in the corner, Miss Trent. You'll be out of the way then. Oh, allow me. A cigarette?
STEVE:	Thank you.
SIR GRAHAM:	Oh, have one of these instead. You'd like them better. (*Chuckles*) These are Russian! They're rather on the strong side.
STEVE:	Russian? Oh, er, would you mind if I tried one?
SIR GRAHAM:	(*Surprised*) No, of course not.
Door opens.	
SERGEANT:	You rang, sir?
SIR GRAHAM:	Oh, yes, tell Inspector Dale and Inspector Merritt and that man Skid Tyler to come in here.
SERGEANT:	Yes, sir.

Door closes.
Long pause.
Door opens.

SIR GRAHAM: (*With authority*) Sit down, Tyler! Er, no, over there!

SKID: What d'ya want? What the 'ell's the idea of dragging me along here? Anyone would think I'm a blasted criminal!

DALE: Be quiet!

SIR GRAHAM: No, that's all right, Dale. Now listen, Tyler, we're going to ask you a few questions, and if you've got any sense you'll tell us the truth. What were you doing in Evesham at the beginning of this week?

SKID: Evesham? Never been near the place.

SIR GRAHAM: My dear fellow, don't for Heaven's sake adopt that attitude. Inspector Merritt saw you there, didn't you, Merritt?

MERRITT: That's right, outside The Little General about three o'clock in the afternoon.

SKID: What would I be doing outside a pub at three o'clock in the afternoon? Now I ask ya!

PAUL TEMPLE: Who said The Little General was a … public house?

SKID: (*Panicky*) Who said so? Why? What? What the hell's this all about? You lot don't know me! You can't hold me here!

PAUL TEMPLE: Last night, my dear fellow, with the aid of a two-ton lorry you accidentally smashed your way into a very select dress shop. By a strange coincidence, the shop next door happened to be a jewellers. By an even

68

	stranger coincidence, it happened to be robbed at precisely the same moment that you decided to make a closer inspection of Madame Isobel's really remarkable exhibition of spring underwear!
SKID:	What you getting' at?
PAUL TEMPLE:	You'll see what I'm getting at, Skid, but first of all tell me … are you fond of children?
SKID:	(*Puzzled*) Children?
PAUL TEMPLE:	You must be. I was forgetting.
SKID:	What the 'ell 'as children got to do with all this?
PAUL TEMPLE:	My dear Skid, you surprise me. Don't you realise … you're holding the baby! And, by Timothy, what a baby!
SKID:	Holding the … Say, listen, if you're trying to be funny then I …
PAUL TEMPLE:	(*Interrupting; confrontational*) I'm not trying to be funny, Skid, I'm an amateur humourist compared with the crowd you've been mixing with.
SKID:	What? What do you mean?
PAUL TEMPLE:	What do I mean? Ha, ha! Our old friend Skid drives the lorry. Our old friend Skid smashed it into a dress shop. Our old friend Skid gets arrested. (*Getting more threatening in tone*) Our old friend Skid visits Scotland Yard! Our old friend Skid …
SKID:	(*Interrupting; in a complete state of hysterical panic*) Shut up! Shut your blasted mouth!

PAUL TEMPLE:	My dear Skid, don't be a darn fool! Why should you take the rap? Why should you …
SKIP:	I'm not talking! I'm not a squealer! I know what's good for me!
PAUL TEMPLE:	You'll talk! And you'll talk fast. (*Quietly*) What were you doing at Evesham? What were you doing near The Little General Inn?
SKID:	I tell ya, I've never been near the place!
PAUL TEMPLE:	Skid, listen! This isn't a one-sided little affair like share pushing. This is big stuff! This is crime with a capital C. And you're in it! In it up to the neck! (*Pause; threateningly*) Now – talk!

A pause.

SKID:	(*Much calmer; having gathered his thoughts*) All right. All right, I'll talk! But first, I – I want a drink. I'm all shot to pieces!
SIR GRAHAM:	All right. I'll get you some brandy. I've got some in the cupboard.

The sound of a drink being poured.

PAUL TEMPLE:	Skid, what is The Green Finger?
SKID:	It's an organisation that … that's been responsible for all the jewel robberies. The Chief of the gang is known as – The Knave of Diamonds!
STEVE:	Max Lorraine!
PAUL TEMPLE:	Have you ever met this person?
SKID:	Leave me alone! Leave me alone! For God's sake leave me alone!
SIR GRAHAM:	Here! Drink this!

SKID starts to cough.

PAUL TEMPLE: Now, Skid, listen, this is important … Have you ever … have you ev…

SKID starts chocking.

PAUL TEMPLE: Skid? Skid!

SIR GRAHAM: What's the matter?

PAUL TEMPLE: Look at him! Skid!

DALE: What is it? He looks so …

MERRITT: (*Interrupting*) Pass me that glass, Sir Graham.

SIR GRAHAM: The glass? But … Good God, you don't mean …!

PAUL TEMPLE: (*Quietly*) He's dead.

STEVE: (*Shocked*) Dead!

DALE: Yes. He's dead all right. What's in the glass, Merritt?

MERRITT: (*Calmly*) Enough cyanide to kill a regiment.

SIR GRAHAM: But – but that's impossible! Why – it was a new bottle! I – I …

Door opens.

SERGEANT: There's a lady to see you, sir, by the name …

SIR GRAHAM: (*Interrupting; hysterical*) I can't see anyone! Tell her I'm out! Tell her to …

PAUL TEMPLE: (*Interrupting*) Just a moment, Sergeant. (*Pause; calmly*) Who is the lady?

SERGEANT: It's a Miss … er … Parchment, sir. A Miss Amelia Victoria Parchment.

END OF EPISODE THREE

EPISODE FOUR

REPLY TO A MURDER

Announcements. Incidental music
Fade music

PAUL TEMPLE:	Now, Skid, listen, this is important … Have you ever … have you ev… Skid? Skid!
SIR GRAHAM:	What's the matter?
PAUL TEMPLE:	Look at him! Skid!
DALE:	What is it? He looks so …
MERRITT:	(*Interrupting*) Pass me that glass, Sir Graham.
SIR GRAHAM:	The glass? But … Good God, you don't mean …!
PAUL TEMPLE:	(*Quietly*) He's dead.
STEVE:	(*Shocked*) Dead!
DALE:	Yes. He's dead all right. What's in the glass, Merritt?
MERRITT:	(*Calmly*) Enough cyanide to kill a regiment.
SIR GRAHAM:	But – but that's impossible! Why – why it was a new bottle! I – I …
Door opens.	
SERGEANT:	There's a lady to see you, sir, by the name …
SIR GRAHAM:	(*Interrupting; hysterical*) I can't see anyone! Tell her I'm out! Tell her to …
PAUL TEMPLE:	(*Interrupting*) Just a moment, Sergeant. (*Pause; calmly*) Who is the lady?
SERGEANT:	It's a Miss … er … Parchment, sir. A Miss Amelia Victoria Parchment.
STEVE:	Miss Parchment!
PAUL TEMPLE:	Ask her to wait a few minutes.
SERGEANT:	Very good, sir.
Door closes.	

DALE:	Where's the bottle, Sir Graham?
SIR GRAHAM:	It's … here … I can't understand it. The bottle's a new one … I bought it myself only two days ago.
DALE:	The stopper doesn't seem to have been tampered with as far as I can see. Just a minute! I'm not so sure!
MERRITT:	Someone must have tampered with it. Why …
PAUL TEMPLE:	(*Interrupting; calmly*) Then the poison must have been meant for you, Sir Graham, and not for Tyler.
SIR GRAHAM:	Yes – it – er – looks very much like it.
MERRITT:	I think we'd better get him into the other room, sir. Then Dr Parkes can have a look at him.
SIR GRAHAM:	Yes … Yes – er – by all means. Oh, and take this bottle. See that Mollinson gets to work on it.
MERRITT:	Yes, sir. Come along, Dale.

Door opens.

SIR GRAHAM:	And tell the doctor I'd like a word with him.
DALE:	Very good, sir.

The sound of MERRITT and DALE removing SKID's body from the room.
Door closes.

SIR GRAHAM:	Terrible business! I can't possibly understand how … I say, I hope it hasn't shaken you up, Miss Trent?
STEVE:	No, I'm all right, Sir Graham. Only I'm afraid I shall have to be going. I have an appointment at four o'clock and I –
SIR GRAHAM:	Yes, of course. Of course.

PAUL TEMPLE: I'll see you later, Steve. About four-thirty?

STEVE: Yes. Goodbye, Sir Graham.

SIR GRAHAM: Goodbye, Miss Trent.

Door opens.

SIR GRAHAM: Oh, Sergeant, Miss Trent is leaving.

SERGEANT: Very good, sir. This way, miss.

Door closes.

SIR GRAHAM: I wonder whether the poison was meant for Tyler, or … or for me?

PAUL TEMPLE: Yes. Yes, I wonder.

SIR GRAHAM: It seems strange that Tyler should be poisoned, just when he was on the point of talking.

PAUL TEMPLE: Yes. Yes, it does seem strange, doesn't it?

SIR GRAHAM: Oh, by the way, Temple, a constable at Leamington remembers talking to a girl in a sports car shortly before the robbery occurred. For some reason or other, he's got it into his head that she had something to do with it.

PAUL TEMPLE: Did he take the number of the car?

SIR GRAHAM: No, I'm afraid he didn't. He's written out a pretty good description of the girl, though. Height about five feet four. Dark. Rather good-looking. Dressed in a small grey costume with a fox fur. She had a set of golf clubs in the back of the car. Oh, and apparently she wore a small black wristlet watch.

PAUL TEMPLE: A small black wristlet watch?

SIR GRAHAM: Yes. Does that convey anything?

PAUL TEMPLE: I don't know. It might.

SIR GRAHAM: We've tried to trace the girl, but so far we've failed.

PAUL TEMPLE: H'm. Sir Graham, I've got an idea in my mind and –

SIR GRAHAM: Yes?

PAUL TEMPLE: There's a jeweller's in Nottingham by the name of "Trenchman". They go in for a considerable number of antiques, and all that sort of thing. I was at Oxford with the junior partner – a fellow called Rice. Alec Rice. Now if it became known that Trenchman's had a very valuable stone on their hands, say a blue-white diamond, for argument's sake, it would be a pretty safe bet that our friends would, in the course of time, pay Trenchman's a friendly little visit.

SIR GRAHAM: Yes. Yes, I dare say they would. Well?

PAUL TEMPLE: Well, I'm of the opinion that the robbery at Leamington, and all the other robberies for that matter, have been very carefully planned and premeditated.

SIR GRAHAM: I still don't quite –

PAUL TEMPLE: (*Interrupting*) I'm also of the definite opinion, Sir Graham, that if it became known, not too well-known mark you, that Trenchman's had a very valuable stone, the people we are up against would take the trouble to verify its existence before actually planning the robbery.

SIR GRAHAM: Verify its existence?

PAUL TEMPLE: Yes. Now Alec Rice would, I feel sure, help us over this matter. He would supply us with a list of all the enquiries they might receive about this particular stone. Naturally, most of them would be quite

78

	legitimate, but there's the possibility, a strong possibility in my opinion, that amongst that list would be an agent of –
SIR GRAHAM:	Of … the Knave of Diamonds!
PAUL TEMPLE:	Yes.
SIR GRAHAM:	By Jove! By Jove! That's an idea, Temple!
PAUL TEMPLE:	Now, the whole idea would have to be handled very, very carefully. We're not dealing with fools, remember. One or two brief references to the stone might appear in the daily press, an article or two in the trade journals, and that's about it. There must be nothing clumsy or blatant about the way the existence of the stone is brought to light, or they'd tumble to the idea immediately.
SIR GRAHAM:	Yes, of course. Excellent idea, Temple! Excellent!
PAUL TEMPLE:	Yes, well, I'll get in touch with Rice immediately.
SIR GRAHAM:	And now I suppose I'd better see this woman, Miss – er – Parchment.
PAUL TEMPLE:	Miss Parchment … did she ask to see you, or –
SIR GRAHAM:	No, I sent for her. She was at the Inn the night Harvey was murdered.
PAUL TEMPLE:	Yes, I know. I questioned her.
SIR GRAHAM:	Oh, did you? She's a retired schoolmistress, isn't she?
PAUL TEMPLE:	Yes. A retired schoolmistress with a passion for old English Inns.
Door opens.	
SERGEANT:	Miss Parchment, sir.

SIR GRAHAM:	I'm sorry to have kept you waiting, Miss Parchment.

Door closes.

SIR GRAHAM:	But I'm rather afraid –
MISS PARCHMENT:	Ah, Mr Temple! How nice to see you again. We meet under pleasanter circumstance this time, I hope. (*Pause*) Or do we?
PAUL TEMPLE:	Yes, of course. And how are you, Miss Parchment? Quite well, I hope?
MISS PARCHMENT:	Oh, quite well, thank you. A little sciatica, you know, now and again but nothing to complain of.
SIR GRAHAM:	Miss Parchment, won't you be seated?
MISS PARCHMENT:	Oh, thank you. Do you know this is the first time I've ever been in Scotland Yard! It's quite thrilling, isn't it?
SIR GRAHAM:	Yes, er, quite thrilling. Will you have a cigarette?
MISS PARCHMENT:	No, thank you, I – Ah! I see you smoke Russian cigarettes!
SIR GRAHAM:	Yes, I – er – prefer them. (*He clears his throat*) Now, Miss Parchment –
MISS PARCHMENT:	(*Interrupting*) So frightfully clever, the Russians, don't you think so, Mr Temple?
PAUL TEMPLE:	Yes, I – er – suppose they are.
MISS PARCHMENT:	Chekhov! Ibsen! (*Pause*) Ibsen? Was Ibsen a Russian? Do you know, I don't think he was! Well, how perfectly extraordinary!
SIR GRAHAM:	Miss Parchment! Miss Parchment, I should like to ask you a few questions.

MISS PARCHMENT: And why not, Sir Graham? And why not?

Long pause.

Door closes.

PAUL TEMPLE: So, this is where you write all those soul-stirring articles for The Evening Post!

STEVE: Well, I'm glad somebody thinks they're soul-stirring! Put those parcels on the table, dear!

PAUL TEMPLE: Right-oh. How long have you been on The Evening Post, Steve?

STEVE: Oh, about eighteen months. I started as "Auntie Mollie".

PAUL TEMPLE: Auntie Mollie?

STEVE: Yes, the – er – the answers to correspondence. You know, the – er – the –

PAUL TEMPLE: Oh, you mean writing articles about – about love – love, and things like that?

STEVE: Mostly about – things like that.

They both laugh awkwardly.

PAUL TEMPLE: I say, this is a grand little place, isn't it?

STEVE: I'm glad you like it.

PAUL TEMPLE: By Timothy, yes! Rather unusual gramophone you've got, Steve.

STEVE: Yes. Gerald bought it for me in Paris the year he –

There is a knock on the door.

Door opens.

STEVE: Ah, tea! I'll help you, Mrs Neddy.

MRS NEDDY: That's all right, dearie. I can manage.

PAUL TEMPLE: Good afternoon.

MRS NEDDY: Good afternoon to you, sir.

STEVE:	Is that parcel for me, Mrs Neddy?
MRS NEDDY:	Parcel? Why, yes, of course. It's a good job you mentioned it now. I should 'ave probably gone to bed with it under me arm!
STEVE:	(*Laughs*) I gather the memory isn't improving?
MRS NEDDY:	Improving! Oh, 'tis something shocking, miss. There are times when I wonder who the Dickens I am!

They both laugh.

STEVE:	Where did the parcel come from, Mrs Neddy? Who delivered it?
MRS NEDDY:	It was delivered about an hour ago, by a boy. A cheeky-faced monkey he was 'an all.
STEVE:	Was there any message?
MRS NEDDY:	No. No message, dearie. Oh Lor, I've forgotten the buttered scones. You'll have to be excusing me, dearier.
	Door opens and closes.
PAUL TEMPLE:	Mrs Neddy seems quite a character.
STEVE:	She's a dear. I wonder what this is.
PAUL TEMPLE:	It looks like a disc of some sort, doesn't it?
STEVE:	Yes. We'll soon find out.

Sound of parcel being unwrapped.

PAUL TEMPLE:	A gramophone record!
STEVE:	I wonder who sent it?
PAUL TEMPLE:	Isn't there some writing on the –

A sharp intake of breath from STEVE.

PAUL TEMPLE:	Steve! Steve, what's the matter?
STEVE:	(*Shocked; shakily*) Look what it says on the record.

PAUL TEMPLE:	To Louise Harvey. From the Knave of Diamonds.
STEVE:	Max Lorraine.
PAUL TEMPLE:	Yes. Steve! What are you going to do?
STEVE:	I'm going to play the record.

The gramophone is switched on.

STEVE:	The set takes a little while to warm up.
PAUL TEMPLE:	Yes.
STEVE:	(*Anxiously*) Paul, what do you think is on the record?
PAUL TEMPLE:	I don't know. Probably a message from – Steve! You're shaking!
STEVE:	No. No, I'm … all right.
PAUL TEMPLE:	Here – I'll put it on. You sit down, dear.

A pause.

STEVE:	What is it, Paul? Why don't you put the record on?
PAUL TEMPLE:	Just a minute. Just a minute! Aren't we being a little obvious, my dear?
STEVE:	A little obvious?
PAUL TEMPLE:	Steve … Supposing you sent someone you knew a record – a gramophone record. It had no official label, and looked very mysterious. What do you think would be the first thing they'd do with it?
STEVE:	Why, play it, of course! That's what everyone would do under the circumstances.
PAUL TEMPLE:	Yes, of course it is. That's what everyone would do under the circumstances.
STEVE:	Paul … I don't understand.
PAUL TEMPLE:	The person who sent you this record knew that you'd be puzzled by it, and he knew, without a shadow of a doubt, that the first

	thing you'd want to do would be to satisfy your curiosity by playing it.
STEVE:	Well?
PAUL TEMPLE:	Steve, don't you see? That's the whole point! The Knave wants you to play this record – and immediately you do so, his purpose in sending it to you is fulfilled!
STEVE:	But – but what is his purpose? Why should he send me a gramophone record? If it contains a message, then–
PAUL TEMPLE:	(*Interrupting*) Any message it contains could have been sent to you in writing.
STEVE:	Yes, I – I suppose it could. Then what's on the record?
PAUL TEMPLE:	Nothing. Nothing of importance. I'm sure of that.
STEVE:	Then why should he send it? You said yourself his purpose was to get me to play it! If nothing is on the record, then –
PAUL TEMPLE:	(*Interrupting*) Yes, why should he send it? By Timothy! By Timothy, Steve! The gramophone!
STEVE:	The gramophone …?
PAUL TEMPLE:	That's what he wants! That's what he wants. He wants you to use the gramophone. Tell me, has it always been in this position?
STEVE:	Yes, always, only–
PAUL TEMPLE:	(*Interrupting*) Well?
STEVE:	It looks as if it might have been moved slightly. It's further against the wall as a rule. Oh, and look at the gauze on the speaker, why–
PAUL TEMPLE:	(*Interrupting*) It's been altered, hasn't it?

84

STEVE: Yes!

PAUL TEMPLE: By Jove, I've got it!

STEVE: (*Anxiously*) What is it?

PAUL TEMPLE: Stand on one side, Steve. Now look, when you want to put a record on, you stand in front of the loud speaker like this, don't you?

STEVE: Yes.

PAUL TEMPLE: And you lift the arm up and bring it across the record?

STEVE: Yes, that's right.

PAUL TEMPLE: I'm going to do exactly the same, only I'm going to stand to one side instead – you'll see why in a minute. Now, stand away, Steve.

The sound of a gunshot rings out.

STEVE TRENT: Paul!

PAUL TEMPLE: There's a small revolver hidden by the speaker. It's been wired up with the tone arm. Immediately the arm was moved, the revolver fired. Now you know why he sent you the gramophone record. Obliging little fellow, isn't he?

STEVE TRENT: Thank goodness you were here when it arrived.

PAUL TEMPLE: Steve, how many people know that your real name is Harvey … Louise Harvey?

STEVE TRENT: Yourself. Lord Broadhedge, the proprietor of The Evening Post, and Sir Graham Forbes. That's all.

PAUL TEMPLE: H'm. And Merritt. Inspector Merritt. I told him myself.

STEVE TRENT: Inspector Merritt?

PAUL TEMPLE: Yes.

STEVE TRENT:	(*Pauses*) What are you thinking of?
PAUL TEMPLE:	I was just wondering how long Sir Graham had smoked Russian cigarettes!

Long pause.
Door closes.

DR MILTON:	Diana!
DIANA:	Has he been through here on the phone?
DR MILTON:	You mean the Chief?
DIANA:	Yes. Yes, of course.
DR MILTON:	No, of course he hasn't. I thought you went to town to see him.
DIANA:	I went to town, all right. I waited over three blasted hours in that tube station, and there wasn't a sign of him.
DR MILTON:	I wonder why he didn't turn up?
DIANA:	I don't know.
DR MILTON:	You haven't heard anything further about Skid?
DIANA:	No. They're still holding him, as far as I know.
DR MILTON:	There's been nothing in the newspapers. I hope to God Skid doesn't talk. That's all I'm worried about.

Door opens.

SNOW:	Any news?
DIANA:	No.
SNOW:	Did you see the Knave?
DIANA:	No!
SNOW:	Somefing's in the wind! Somefing's in the wind, if you ask me!
DIANA:	Well, nobody's asking you!

SNOW: It's been three days since the robbery and we haven't heard a word about Skid. I tell you, he'll talk! He'll talk!

DR MILTON: Shut up, Snow! Have you seen Horace?

SNOW: Yus.

DR MILTON: What about the stuff?

SNOW: That's all right. That's all right.

DR MILTON: Then there's nothing to worry about! Mix me a drink, and you'd better mix yourself one too.

The telephone begins to ring.

SNOW: The phone.

DR MILTON: That's the Chief! It's the special line.

DIANA: Yes. I'll take it.

                  The telephone receiver is lifted.

DIANA: Hello … Hello … Yes … Why didn't you meet me? … What? Yes … Yes. I'm listening …

DR MILTON: What is it?

DIANA: Sshh! … Yes … When? … Temple? … Yes … Yes … I say, be careful! … The Doc's here now … Yes … Yes, all right. Goodbye.

The telephone receiver is replaced.

DR MILTON: Well?

SNOW: How's Skid?

DIANA: Skid's dead!

DR MILTON: Dead!

DIANA: Yes. He was going to – talk.

DR MILTON: He … he didn't?

DIANA: No. The Knave stopped him in time.

DR MILTON: Why didn't he meet you?

DIANA: I don't know, he didn't say. You'd better get in touch with Horace, Snow! Tell him we meet again on Friday.

SNOW:	Friday?
DR MILTON:	Why so early?
DIANA:	There's a jewellers at Nottingham called Trenchman. They've got a new stone. The Chief wants me to have a look at it. I'm going over there tomorrow. If it's as good as the reports say it is, then … we'll discuss the matter on Friday with Dixie.
DR MILTON:	Good.
DIANA:	Oh, and there's just one other point. Our friend Mr Paul Temple has got to be taken care of. Do you think you can manage it, Doc?
DR MILTON:	What do you think? (*He chuckles*) What do you think?

Long pause.

STEVE TRENT:	Your Aunty's quite a hearty individual!
PAUL TEMPLE:	Hearty's hardly the word! What is it, Pryce?
PRYCE:	Mr Alec Rice has called to see you, sir.
PAUL TEMPLE:	Oh, good! Show him in! This is the jeweller from Nottingham. The chap I was telling you about, remember? I – um – oh, hello, Alec, how are you?
ALEC RICE:	Oh, fine old boy! You're looking fit.
PAUL TEMPLE:	Er, Miss Trent – Mr Alec Rice.
ALEC RICE:	How do you do?
STEVE TRENT:	How do you do?
ALEC RICE:	Er – I'm in rather a hurry, Paul, but I – er – I – er – happened to be passing …
PAUL TEMPLE:	Oh, that's all right, Alec. You can speak in front of Miss Trent.

ALEC RICE:	Oh, good. Well, your little publicity stunt about the "Trenchman" diamond seems to be working out all right. We've certainly had plenty of inquiries.
PAUL TEMPLE:	Oh?
ALEC RICE:	Most of them, of course, are quite legitimate.
PAUL TEMPLE:	Yes.
ALEC RICE:	People in the trade. People we've dealt with for years. But this morning, about eleven o'clock, I think it was about eleven, a girl came into the shop.
PAUL TEMPLE:	Yes?
ALEC RICE:	She asked to see some statuettes we had in the window; she examined one or two, and eventually bought one. Just before she was leaving, however, she asked to see your stone. She said she'd read something about it in one of the newspapers.
PAUL TEMPLE:	Go on.
ALEC RICE:	Well, there's nothing more to tell, really. She admired the diamond we showed her and, and that was the finish of it.
PAUL TEMPLE:	What did she look like?
ALEC RICE:	Dark! Sort of – sort of voluptuous!

STEVE *laughs*.

PAUL TEMPLE:	Er – good looking?
ALEC RICE:	Yes. Yes, I suppose she was.
PAUL TEMPLE:	Well, something must have impressed you about her, or you wouldn't –
ALEC RICE:	(*Interrupting*) As a matter of fact, old boy, I got the impression that all this business about the statuettes was a sort of – was a sort of a blind, you know. I think the real

89

reason for her visit was to have a jolly good "decko" at the diamond.

PAUL TEMPLE: Was she tall?

ALEC RICE: Mm – I suppose she was.

PAUL TEMPLE: You don't seem to have been very observant!

ALEC RICE: Good Lord, old boy – you can hardly … I say, just a minute! I tell you what I did notice. She had a rather snappy wristlet watch. Looked to me as if it was made of onyx or something. It was–

PAUL TEMPLE: (*Interrupting; quietly*) It was black, with a diamond clasp, and a small platinum safety chain.

ALEC RICE: Yes, yes! I say, do you know the girl?

PAUL TEMPLE: I think perhaps I do, Alec. I think perhaps I do.

ALEC RICE: Oh well, I must be toddling!

PAUL TEMPLE: Look here, won't you stop and have a drink or something?

ALEC RICE: Sorry, old boy – in a frightful hurry!

PAUL TEMPLE: You appear you must – er …

Door opens.

PAUL TEMPLE: Show Mr Rice out, will you, Pryce?

PRYCE: Come this way, if you please, sir.

Door closes.

STEVE TRENT: Did you – er – know the girl he was talking about?

PAUL TEMPLE: Yes. Her name is Thornley. Diana Thornley. Miss Thornley and her uncle, Dr Milton, dined with me about a fortnight ago.

STEVE TRENT: And you noticed the wristlet watch?

90

PAUL TEMPLE: Yes, I noticed it. And so did Alec. And so did the constable at Leamington. Do you know, Steve, I think it might be quite a good idea if we paid Dr Milton a visit.

Long pause.
STEVE TRENT: I should ring again.
The sound of the doorbell ringing.
PAUL TEMPLE: There doesn't seem to be anyone in, as far as I – Just a minute!
The door is unlocked from the inside.
PAUL TEMPLE: Ah, good evening!
SNOW: Good evening, sir.
PAUL TEMPLE: I should like to see Dr Milton. My name is –
SNOW: (*Interrupting*) Dr Milton is out. He went into Evesham about an hour ago.
PAUL TEMPLE: Oh. Oh, I see. Er, then perhaps Miss Thornley would –
SNOW: (*Interrupting*) Miss Thornley is with the doctor, sir.
PAUL TEMPLE: Oh. Er, that's rather unfortunate, isn't it?
SNOW: Was the doctor expecting you, sir?
PAUL TEMPLE: No. No, I don't think he was. Still, if he's only popped into Evesham, it might be quite a good idea if we waited.
SNOW: I 'ardly think the doctor will be back for quite a little while, sir.
PAUL TEMPLE: Oh. Oh, er, don't you? Still, I think we'll wait.
SNOW: Very good, sir. This way, if you please.
Door closes.
Door opens.
PAUL TEMPLE: Ah, thank you.

SNOW: This is the lounge, sir. I'll let you know
                   immediately the doctor returns.

PAUL TEMPLE: Splendid!

SNOW: What name shall I –

PAUL TEMPLE: (*Interrupting*) Temple. Paul Temple.

SNOW: Temple? Oh, thank you, sir.

Door closes.

STEVE TRENT: M'm, well, I don't think Boris Karloff
                   would keep him awake.

PAUL TEMPLE: (*Laughs*) Behind that rough exterior there
                   probably lurks a heart of gold.

STEVE TRENT: Lurks is about right, if you ask me!

PAUL TEMPLE: (*Chuckles*) I say, it's a pretty impressive
                   sort of place, this, isn't it?

STEVE TRENT: Yes. Our friend, the doctor, certainly
                   believes in statues. There's eight on the
                   mantlepiece.

PAUL TEMPLE: There's nothing particularly modest about
                   them, either.

PAUL and STEVE giggle.

PAUL TEMPLE: Hello, hello!

STEVE TRENT: What is it?

PAUL TEMPLE: Dear, oh dear. It looks as if our friend Mr
                   Karloff was spinning a little story when he
                   said the doctor and Diana left an hour ago.

STEVE TRENT: Why?

PAUL TEMPLE: There's a cigarette-end in the fireplace and
                   it obviously hasn't been there very long
                   either, judging from appearances.

STEVE TRENT: Perhaps the butler was having a quiet little
                   smoke. That would account for him
                   keeping us waiting.

PAUL TEMPLE: It wouldn't account for the lip rouge on the cigarette, dearie! Unless we've greatly misjudged our friend.

STEVE TRENT: I say, Paul …

PAUL TEMPLE: Yes?

STEVE TRENT: This is a funny sort of thing, isn't it?

PAUL TEMPLE: What is it?

STEVE TRENT: I don't know. Looks like a statue of something or other …

PAUL TEMPLE: I wouldn't touch it.

STEVE TRENT: The top part is quite loose. It's …

A wall panel begins to move.

STEVE TRENT: Paul, look! Look!

PAUL TEMPLE: By Timothy, it's part of the panelling in the wall! You must have opened it when you twisted the statue.

STEVE TRENT: Yes!

PAUL TEMPLE: No, don't touch the statue, Steve. We must have a look at this.

Pause.

STEVE TRENT: Can you see anything?

PAUL TEMPLE: Yes. It's just a small room – nothing exciting about it. It's not even furnished.

STEVE TRENT: Oh.

PAUL TEMPLE: Let's have a look inside.

PAUL squeezes through the gap the open panel has created.

PAUL TEMPLE: There we are. Come on, Steve! Can you get in all right?

STEVE TRENT: Yes.

PAUL TEMPLE: That's better. Not very impressive, is it?

STEVE TRENT: It doesn't seem to be used at all as far as I can see. Isn't there a light?

PAUL TEMPLE: Yes, but I'm blowed if I can see the switch. Close the panel, Steve. I have an idea that might work it.

STEVE TRENT: Right.

STEVE pushes the panel closed.

STEVE TRENT: Yes.

PAUL TEMPLE: I thought it would. I could see the small notch on the corner of –

A sound like that of a lift descending starts.

PAUL TEMPLE: What's that?

The sound gets louder.

STEVE TRENT: It sounds like … Paul! The panel won't open!

PAUL TEMPLE: Budge up! Here, let me try. Gosh, you're right! We're locked in! Listen!

STEVE TRENT: Paul! Paul! We're moving!

PAUL TEMPLE: Moving?

STEVE TRENT: It's the room – can't you feel it? Can't you feel it?

PAUL TEMPLE: Yes! Yes! By Timothy, Steve, we're in a lift!

STEVE TRENT: A lift!

PAUL TEMPLE: Keep still!

STEVE TRENT: Paul! We're going down! We're – going – down! We're – going – down!!!

END OF EPISODE FOUR

EPISODE FIVE

ACTION AT THE INN

Announcements. Fade music.

STEVE TRENT: Can you see anything?

PAUL TEMPLE: Yes. It's just a small room – nothing exciting about it. It's not even furnished.

STEVE TRENT: Oh.

PAUL TEMPLE: Let's have a look inside.

PAUL squeezes through the gap the open panel has created.

PAUL TEMPLE: There we are. Come on, Steve! Can you get in all right?

STEVE TRENT: Yes.

PAUL TEMPLE: That's better. Not very impressive, is it?

STEVE TRENT: It doesn't seem to be used at all as far as I can see. Isn't there a light?

PAUL TEMPLE: Yes, but I'm blowed if I can see the switch. Close the panel, Steve. I have an idea that might work it.

STEVE TRENT: Right.

STEVE pushes the panel closed.

STEVE TRENT: Yes.

PAUL TEMPLE: I thought it would. I could see the small notch on the corner of –

A sound like that of a lift descending starts.

PAUL TEMPLE: What's that?

The sound gets louder.

STEVE TRENT: Paul! Paul! We're moving!

PAUL TEMPLE: Moving?

STEVE TRENT: It's the room – can't you feel it? Can't you feel it?

PAUL TEMPLE: Yes! Yes! By Timothy, Steve, we're in a lift!

STEVE TRENT: A lift!

PAUL TEMPLE: Keep still!

STEVE TRENT: Paul! We're going down! We're – going – down! We're – going – down!!!

The sound continues and then eventually begins to wind down.

PAUL TEMPLE: We're stopping, Steve …

STEVE TRENT: Yes.

The noise fades completely.

PAUL TEMPLE: Open the panel, Steve.

STEVE TRENT: (*Nervously*) I wonder where we are.

PAUL TEMPLE: Probably the bargain basement. Here, I'll try that.

PAUL rolls another panel open.

STEVE TRENT: Looks like a passage of some sort.

PAUL TEMPLE: Yes. Can you get out all right?

STEVE TRENT: I think so. They don't give you much room, do they?

A pause.

PAUL TEMPLE: I wonder where this place leads to.

STEVE TRENT: I've got a pretty awful sense of direction, but we seem to be going towards the village, as far as I can make out.

PAUL TEMPLE: Yes! We'll walk to the end.

STEVE TRENT: Yes, all right.

PAUL TEMPLE: Can you see?

STEVE TRENT: Not too badly.

PAUL TEMPLE: This passage is pretty old. It must have been here for donkey's years.

STEVE TRENT: Yes.

PAUL TEMPLE: Seems fairly long, doesn't it?

STEVE TRENT: Paul! Paul, there's a light?

PAUL TEMPLE: Where? Oh, yes.

STEVE TRENT: It's an oil lamp. Someone must have been here quite recently.

PAUL TEMPLE: Someone's been here quite recently, all right. Don't worry about that. I wonder where the devil this leads to?

STEVE TRENT: Most probably The Little General. Everything seems –

PAUL TEMPLE: (*Interrupting*) By Timothy, Steve, you're right! You're right!

STEVE TRENT: Why, Paul, you don't –

PAUL TEMPLE: (*Interrupting*) The Little General lies about a hundred yards from Ashdown House. We must have come fifty yards already –

STEVE TRENT: (*Interrupting*) Then, then you really think this passage leads towards the Inn?

PAUL TEMPLE: We'll soon find out. We'll soon find out, Steve.

Dramatic incidental music crashes in.
A pause.

STEVE TRENT: There's some sort of a wooden staircase over there.

PAUL TEMPLE: Yes. We're underneath the Inn, all right. I don't think there's any doubt about that.

The muffled sound of voices in the distance is heard.

PAUL TEMPLE: Can you hear voices?

STEVE TRENT: Yes. Yes, I think I can.

PAUL TEMPLE: If we climb to the top of the staircase we might hear.

STEVE TRENT: Yes.

PAUL TEMPLE: Be careful, Steve.

Floor boards on the stairs start to creak.

PAUL TEMPLE: Ssh!

STEVE TRENT: Paul, listen. Listen …

DIANA: (*Fade in*) … the Doc to tell you what to do.

DALEY: What's happened to Skid?

DR MILTON: He's dead.

DALEY: Dead! I thought you said the smash was –

DR MILTON: (*Interrupting*) It wasn't the smash, Horace.

DALEY: Then what was it?

DR MILTON: He had to be taken care of.

DALEY: Taken – care – of. You don't mean the Knave–

DR MILTON: Yes.

DALEY: Why should he? Why should Skid be murdered?

DR MILTON: He had to go. He was on the point of talking.

DALEY: How do we know he was on the point of talking?

DIXIE: That's what I say!

DALEY: It was the same with Snipey Jackson and Lefty. They did their job well and then look what …

DR MILTON: Jackson was a fool. And an incompetent fool into the bargain. He didn't even wear gloves on the Leicester job.

DALEY: And what about Lefty?

DR MILTON: That was my fault. I was sorry about that. I only meant to give the poor devil a whiff of chloroform and he passed out on me.

DALEY: Yes, well, it sounds all right. But I'm just getting a bit windy. The Knave is just a little too smart for my liking.

DIANA: A little too smart, eh, Horace? How very interesting.

DR MILTON: If the Knave wasn't smart, we shouldn't be here, my friend, you can take that from me.

DALEY: What d'ya mean?

100

DR MILTON: The Knave received information about a valuable diamond owned by a Nottingham firm called Trenchman's. Diana went round there this morning and had a look at it. We were supposed to make all the arrangements about the job tonight. But this morning, after Diana got back, the Chief rang up, and ...

DALEY: Well?

DR MILTON: The Trenchman diamond was a trap – a charming little noose, my friend, for us all to put our pretty little necks in.

DALEY: Strewth! What about Diana? How do we know she wasn't follered?

DIANA: I may have been.

DR MILTON: We don't know. Diana's got to lie low for a while.

DIXIE: It's a damn good job the Chief found out about Trenchman's or we should 'ave been in a well jam.

DALEY: Whose idea was it to have a plant like that? I bet a fiver it –

DR MILTON: (*Interrupting*) It was Mr Paul Temple's idea, unless I'm very much mistaken. And, unless I'm very much mistaken, Mr Temple is going to be aptly rewarded for his originality.

DIXIE: Then Heaven help the poor devil if you get your hands on him, Doc. D'you remember that Greek feller ... and the small drops of acid? I'll never forget his face. He was –

DALEY: (*Panicky*) Shut up! Shut up!

DR MILTON laughs.

DIANA: Horace is a little sensitive. Aren't you, Horace?

DALEY: I saw him, and you didn't! He was staring – staring!

DR MILTON: Pull yourself together, Horace! Now listen, and listen carefully … The Chief's got another idea up his sleeve, and as far as I can make out, it's going to be a pretty big proposition. He wants you all here, in Room 7, on Thursday, at nine sharp.

DALEY: Is – is he coming?

DR MILTON: Yes. Yes, he's coming. Dixie, I want you to meet Snow at the house. I'll see he gets his instructions. (*Start fade out*) You can come down the passage until you reach …

STEVE TRENT: Paul! We'd better go back to the house.

PAUL TEMPLE: Yes. Careful, Steve.

STEVE TRENT: Do you think we should be able to work the lift?

PAUL TEMPLE: We'll have to. Mind that bottom step.

STEVE TRENT: You can see quite clearly when you get used to the light.

PAUL TEMPLE: Yes. Now, come on, Steve, we must hurry!

Incidental music plays in.

STEVE TRENT: Here we are.

PAUL TEMPLE: This panel is … Ah! That's got it!

Sound of panel opening.

PAUL TEMPLE: Hurry, Steve.

Sound of panel closing.

The sound of the lift ascending.

STEVE TRENT: It's working. We're going up!

PAUL TEMPLE: Yes. I hope Karloff the butler hasn't missed us.

The sound of the lift plays for a long time finally slowly winding down as the lift comes to a halt.

STEVE TRENT: Is – is the room empty?

PAUL TEMPLE: Yes.

STEVE TRENT: Good.

PAUL TEMPLE: Careful.

Long pause.

PAUL TEMPLE: That's fine. Now, how do we close the panel from the … Oh, the statue, Steve.

STEVE TRENT: I'll do it.

Sound of the panel closing.

PAUL TEMPLE: Good.

STEVE TRENT: Now what?

PAUL TEMPLE: Steve, Steve, I'm worried.

STEVE TRENT: Worried? Why?

PAUL TEMPLE: I'm worried because you're mixed up in this affair. These people are dangerous. They'll stop at nothing. You've got to watch yourself, Steve. You've got to watch yourself!

STEVE TRENT: Don't worry. I will. You're very sweet.

PAUL TEMPLE: Ever since that incident in your flat … with the record … I've been anxious for you. Steve, can't you go away for a little while? Take –

STEVE TRENT: (*Interrupting*) No! No, and even if I could – I shouldn't. This is my affair, Paul – my affair more than anyone else's – the Knave of Diamonds killed my brother and I –

PAUL TEMPLE: (*Interrupting*) But, Steve, you must –

STEVE TRENT: (*Interrupting*) But that isn't everything. The whole affair is much deeper than that, Paul … much deeper. From the very beginning of the Cape Town robberies eight years ago I knew, and hated, the name of Max Lorraine. I knew that sooner or later I should have to face him. Please believe me, Paul, when I –

103

PAUL TEMPLE: (*Interrupting*) Steve, listen! We agreed that it would be Paul Temple versus Max Lorraine – and that's what it's got to be. You heard them talking in that room at the Inn: and you know the type of people we're up against. Steve, for my sake – you've got to keep out of this.

STEVE TRENT: But, Paul …

PAUL TEMPLE: I shall make a point of seeing Sir Graham first thing tomorrow morning. That Inn must be raided on Thursday at all costs. Steve, there's something I've been wanting to ask you.

STEVE TRENT: Well?

PAUL TEMPLE: You remember you told me when your brother was investigating the Cape Town robberies he worked with another officer. A man who was later murdered by Max Lorraine.

STEVE TRENT: Yes. Yes, that's right.

PAUL TEMPLE: Tell me. What did they call the man?

STEVE TRENT: Er – Bellman. Sydney Bellman. Why?

PAUL TEMPLE: I was just wondering. That's all.

STEVE TRENT: Are we going to wait here …

PAUL TEMPLE: No! I think we've seen enough of Ashdown House for the time being. I'll get hold of this butler fellow and tell him we're not waiting. Is that the bell push?

STEVE TRENT: Yes. I'll ring.

A pause. The distant sound of a door closing.

PAUL TEMPLE: He's coming.

Door opens.

SNOW: You rang, sir?

PAUL TEMPLE: Yes. We've decided not to wait for Dr Milton. Perhaps you'd be kind enough to give him my regards?

SNOW: Certainly, sir. (*Begin fade*) Good night, sir. Good night, Miss!

Pause.

SIR GRAHAM: (*Fade in*) By gosh, it was a lucky chance that Miss Trent touched that statue. You say this passage runs from the doctor's house into the actual Inn itself?

PAUL TEMPLE: Yes, Sir Graham.

SIR GRAHAM: M'm. Do you think this passage is a recent innovation or –

PAUL TEMPLE: (*Interrupting*) No. It's been there for donkey's years: it must have been. I daresay it was used by smugglers originally as a sort of storing house. Why, some of these old English inns have –

SIR GRAHAM: What is it?

PAUL TEMPLE: (*Quietly*) I was thinking. I wonder if Miss Parchment knew there was a definite connection between the doctor's house and The Little General?

SIR GRAHAM: Miss Parchment? Who's Miss Parchment? (*Chuckles*) Oh, the retired school mistress! Good heavens, why should she know anything about it?

PAUL TEMPLE: I – er, just wondered, that's all.

SIR GRAHAM: You know, the thing that beats me, Temple, is how this fellow, the, er, Knave of Diamonds, discovered that the Trenchman affair was a trap.

PAUL TEMPLE:	Well, the answer to that is quite simple, Sir Graham.
SIR GRAHAM:	Quite simple?
PAUL TEMPLE:	The Knave is here! Amongst us! He knows all our plans, and everything about us.
SIR GRAHAM:	Good God, Temple! Are you suggesting –
PAUL TEMPLE:	(*Interrupting*) I'm suggesting nothing, Sir Graham, that the facts themselves do not indicate. Skid Tyler was murdered, remember, here, in this very office, because he was on the point of divulging the identity of the Knave of Diamonds.
SIR GRAHAM:	Yes. Yes, you're right, Temple. Then who is the Knave?
PAUL TEMPLE:	(*Quietly*) I don't know. But I may have a pretty good idea within twenty-four hours.
SIR GRAHAM:	Within twenty-four hours?
PAUL TEMPLE:	Yes. There's a meeting to be held at The Little General tomorrow night at nine. And the Knave will be there!
SIR GRAHAM:	Then –
PAUL TEMPLE:	(*Interrupting*) I want about a dozen of your men to surround the place. If anyone attempts to leave, have them picked up. But no one must be stopped from entering the Inn, do you understand?
SIR GRAHAM:	Yes. And the doctor's house?
PAUL TEMPLE:	Exactly the same precautions must be taken. At about 9.15, the men watching the house will close in on it – force an entrance – and come down the underground passage to the Inn. Is that clear?

SIR GRAHAM: Yes.

PAUL TEMPLE: Meanwhile, at 9.15, the men watching the Inn follow exactly the same procedure: close in on The Little General and force an entrance.

SIR GRAHAM: Yes. Yes!

There is a knock on the door.

Door opens.

DALE: Oh, I'm sorry, sir. I thought –

SIR GRAHAM: That's all right, Dale! Tell Davis of the Flying Squad I want a word with him.

DALE: Very good, sir.

Door closes.

PAUL TEMPLE: I should have your men planted by about eight, Sir Graham, and then –

SIR GRAHAM: (*Interrupting*) Now, don't worry. I'll see to that all right.

PAUL TEMPLE: Good.

SIR GRAHAM: It might be a good idea if I came down myself! The two of us could join the men at The Little General, and then –

PAUL TEMPLE: (*Interrupting*) Yes! Yes, splendid!

SIR GRAHAM: By gosh, Temple, we've got him! We've got him this time!

PAUL TEMPLE: I wonder, Sir Graham.

Long pause.

PAUL TEMPLE: Are the men armed, Sir Graham?

SIR GRAHAM: Some of them are, I believe, aren't they, Dale?

DALE: The men watching the house have service revolvers, sir. I thought under the circumstances that –

SIR GRAHAM: (*Interrupting*) Oh, of course. Yes, yes!

PAUL TEMPLE:	You understand about the statue, don't you, Inspector?
DALE:	Yes, I think so, sir. It's on the left you say, as soon as you enter the lounge?
PAUL TEMPLE:	Yes, that's right. The head of the statue is on a sort of base: as soon as you turn it, you'll see the panel in the wall. I told you about the light, didn't I?
DALE:	Yes.
PAUL TEMPLE:	As far as I could gather, the lift works automatically. Immediately you close the panel you'll hear the machinery.
DALE:	I see.
SIR GRAHAM:	I think someone ought to be left behind in the house, Dale. I should leave Smith, Hodgson, and Mowbray. We'll pick them up later.
DALE:	Very good, sir.
SIR GRAHAM:	By the way, you have the search warrant?
DALE:	Oh, yes, sir!
SIR GRAHAM:	Good. Well, I think that's about all, isn't it, Temple?
PAUL TEMPLE:	Yes. We shall we waiting for you at The Little General. Good luck!
DALE:	Thank you, sir.
SIR GRAHAM:	And be careful in that passage. I expect the devils know the place backwards.
DALE:	Well, even if they get past me, sir, Mowbray and company will be waiting for them in the lounge.
SIR GRAHAM:	Oh, yes, of course! Right, Dale, good luck!
DALE:	Thank you, sir.

Door closes.

PAUL TEMPLE:	He seems a nice fellow – Dale.

SIR GRAHAM: Yes. A bit reserved, but very efficient. He's only been at the Yard about twelve months.

PAUL TEMPLE: Oh.

SIR GRAHAM: What time is it exactly?

PAUL TEMPLE: I make it – er – 8.40.

SIR GRAHAM: How long should it take us to get down to the Inn?

PAUL TEMPLE: Oh, about fifteen minutes. No longer.

SIR GRAHAM: Oh, well, there's no hurry.

PAUL TEMPLE: Dale said he had six men at the house. How many are watching the Inn?

SIR GRAHAM: Now let me see. There's Foster, Robinson … Oh, about eight or nine, I should say.

PAUL TEMPLE: Good. Is Merritt there?

SIR GRAHAM: No.

PAUL TEMPLE: Then I think the best plan would be for you and me to enter the Inn first. Then if possible, we can also –

Door opens.

PAUL TEMPLE: Oh, what is it, Pryce?

PRYCE: There's a lady called to see you, sir. A Mrs Neddy. I told her you were engaged, but –

PAUL TEMPLE: (*Interrupting*) Mrs Neddy? Good Lord, that's Steve's landlady; surely she –

MRS NEDDY: (*Bursting in and interrupting*) You'll have to excuse me bursting in on you like this, Mr Temple. Oh, dear. Oh, dear, I'm that exhausted.

PAUL TEMPLE: Sit down, Mrs Neddy. Oh, that's all right, Pryce.

PRYCE: Very good, sir.

MRS NEDDY: I'm sorry to be troubling you, sir, but –

Door closes.

PAUL TEMPLE:	Now, that's all right. Just take your time.
MRS NEDDY:	Thank you, sir. Ah! Oh, what a relief!
PAUL TEMPLE:	(*Slight pause*) Now, do you feel any better?
MRS NEDDY:	Ah! Oh, yes. Yes, very much better, thank you, sir.
PAUL TEMPLE:	Good. Now, what it is you wanted to see me about?
MRS NEDDY:	It's about – about Miss Trent, sir.
PAUL TEMPLE:	(*Quietly*) Miss Trent? What about Miss Trent?
MRS NEDDY:	She's … she's disappeared, sir.
SIR GRAHAM:	Disappeared!
PAUL TEMPLE:	What makes you say that, Mrs Neddy?
MRS NEDDY:	Well, it's like this, sir. This morning at about half-past nine, the telephone rang in Miss Trent's flat. I was in the kitchen downstairs at the time, and I could 'ear it as clear as a bell, as you might say, sir. I can always hear the telephone, sir, because with the kitchen being rather on the –
PAUL TEMPLE:	(*Interrupting*) Yes, yes, Mrs Neddy, but what happened?
MRS NEDDY:	Well, sir, after a little while, Miss Trent comes downstairs. She seemed in rather a hurry, and a bit excited. I asked her if she was going out, and whether she'd be back for lunch or not. I always likes to know if she'll be in for lunch, sir, because you see –
PAUL TEMPLE:	(*Impatiently*) Yes, yes. What did she say, Mrs Neddy?
MRS NEDDY:	She said that the editor 'ad sent for her and she'd probably be back in about an hour

110

and a nalf. She also asked me not to turn her room out since she'd probably want to stay in all day and work. It very often happens with Miss Trent, sir. She goes down to the newspaper office –

PAUL TEMPLE: (*Interrupting*) Yes, yes. Go on, Mrs Neddy. Please.

MRS NEDDY: Well, sir, there's nothing much to tell, really, except that – she never came back. And then, about a quarter to twelve – the telephone went again. I could hear it all over the blessed house … So, after a while, I went upstairs and answered it, and … and –

PAUL TEMPLE: Yes, Mrs Neddy!

MRS NEDDY: It was the newspaper office, sir. They said they wanted to speak to Miss Trent. I told them she had left the house immediately after they called her. But, but … well, the man at the other end, he said he was the editor, and that – that …

PAUL TEMPLE: Yes?

MRS NEDDY: (*Incredulously*) That they never had called her.

PAUL TEMPLE: Good Lord!

MRS NEDDY: I – I didn't know what to do, sir. I was in a quandairy, as you might say. Then suddenly I remember all those articles Miss Trent used to write about – "Send For Paul Temple", and I thought – I thought …

PAUL TEMPLE: You acted very wisely, Mrs Neddy, very wisely.

111

SIR GRAHAM: Temple, you don't think that the Knave
                …?
PAUL TEMPLE: (*Interrupting*) Yes. By Timothy, we've no
                time to lose, Sir Graham. No time to lose!
Melodramatic incidental music crashes in.

SIR GRAHAM: Anything to report, Turner?
TURNER: No, sir.
PAUL TEMPLE: Has anyone entered the Inn?
TURNER: Not a soul, sir; I can't understand it.
PAUL TEMPLE: Come along, Sir Graham.
SIR GRAHAM: You know the signal, Turner? In case we
                need you.
TURNER: Yes, sir.
Door opens.
SIR GRAHAM: The place seems deserted.
PAUL TEMPLE: Yes. I wonder if there's anyone in the back
                parlour?
SIR GRAHAM: We'll soon find out.
Door opens.
PAUL TEMPLE: Ah. No, it looks to me as if we're on a
                wild goose chase.
SIR GRAHAM: Where does this door lead to?
PAUL TEMPLE: Oh, that door leads outside, I think, into a
                sort of courtyard. You won't find anything
                out there except pigeons.
SIR GRAHAM: Well, where the devil is the room you
                were telling me about? Room 7?
PAUL TEMPLE: Yes. That's what I want to know.
SIR GRAHAM: It can't very well be upstairs, because of
                the passage leading from the house.
PAUL TEMPLE: No … It must be behind this panelling.
PAUL knocks on the panelling.
PAUL TEMPLE: Somewhere …

PAUL continues to knock.

SIR GRAHAM: It sounds solid enough.

PAUL TEMPLE: Yes, but there's quite a gap between this parlour and the staircase. I reckon that's where the room is.

SIR GRAHAM: Yes, but how are we going to get into it? There must be some –

PAUL TEMPLE: (*Interrupting*) Just a minute!

SIR GRAHAM: What is it?

PAUL TEMPLE: I thought I heard … Listen!

SIR GRAHAM: There's someone behind the panelling!

PAUL TEMPLE: Yes.

Suddenly knocking starts from the other side of the panelling. It's in a pattern.

SIR GRAHAM: That's Dale!

PAUL TEMPLE: By Timothy, he's been quick!

SIR GRAHAM: Is that you, Dale?

DALE: (*From the other side of the panelling*) Yes. Where are you?

PAUL TEMPLE: Knock on the wall, Dale!

DALE repeats the coded knocking.

SIR GRAHAM: He's over here, I think.

PAUL TEMPLE: There must be some way to get –

SIR GRAHAM: (*Interrupting*) Look! The panel's moving.

The sound of the panel opening.

PAUL TEMPLE: He must have found the switch!

SIR GRAHAM: Yes.

DALE: Hello, Sir Graham. There's a room in here, sir; it seems …

PAUL TEMPLE: Yes, that's what we're looking for. Mind your head on that beam.

SIR GRAHAM: Oh, thank you.

DALE: I was certainly lucky to find the switch for the panel.

113

PAUL TEMPLE:	So … this … is Room 7!
SIR GRAHAM:	Where's the entrance from the house?
DALE:	Through that cupboard, sir. There's another panel. It leads down to the passage.
SIR GRAHAM:	H'm. Well, these people certainly picked a good hideout. Did you find anyone in the house, Dale?
DALE:	No, sir. But on the small table in the hall I found this.
SIR GRAHAM:	What is it?
PAUL TEMPLE:	It's a playing card. The Knave of Diamonds.
DALE:	There's something on the back, sir.
PAUL TEMPLE:	By Timothy!
SIR GRAHAM:	What does it say?
PAUL TEMPLE:	It says, "Enter Paul Temple … Exit … Louise Harvey".
SIR GRAHAM:	Exit … Louise Harvey. Temple! We've got to find that girl!
DALE:	Sir Graham!
SIR GRAHAM:	What is it?
DALE:	There's someone in the back parlour! Look, you can see his head –
PAUL TEMPLE:	(*Interrupting*) Why, it's Merritt! Come in, Charles!
MERRITT:	Hello, Paul. What the devil do you …? Sir Graham! Good evening, sir.
SIR GRAHAM:	Evening, Merritt. What are you doing here?
MERRITT:	I came down to see Mr Temple, sir. His man told me he was at The Little General and – well, it's lucky you're here, too, sir.
SIR GRAHAM:	Why? What is it, Merritt?

114

MERRITT:	I'm afraid I've got bad news, sir.
SIR GRAHAM:	Bad news?
MERRITT:	It's Radcliffe and Chambers, of Malvern, sir. They rang through this evening –
PAUL TEMPLE:	(*Interrupting; urgently*) Radcliffe and Chambers? You mean the jewellery people?
MERRITT:	Aye.
SIR GRAHAM:	Merritt! You don't mean to say that there's been another robbery?
MERRITT:	Yes, Sir Graham. £14,000 worth.
SIR GRAHAM:	Fourteen thousand – Good Lord, Merritt, why –
PAUL TEMPLE:	(*Interrupting*) When did this happen?
MERRITT:	About six o'clock. Apparently, a man went into the shop and … Oh, by the way, Paul. Pryce asked me to give you this cable. It arrived about five minutes after you left.
PAUL TEMPLE:	Good! I've been expecting this. Excuse me, will you?

PAUL tears open the cable.

PAUL TEMPLE:	Ah! Interesting news, Sir Graham. It's from a friend of mine in South Africa. He's attached to the Cape Town Intelligence Department.
SIR GRAHAM:	Well, what does he say?
PAUL TEMPLE:	He says, "Sydney Bellman was unmarried, but he had a sister".
SIR GRAHAM:	Who the devil is Sydney Bellman?
PAUL TEMPLE:	He was the man who assisted Harvey when he was in South Africa. They worked together over what was known as the Simonstown Case.

SIR GRAHAM:	Oh, yes, I remember. Didn't Miss Trent say he was murdered?
PAUL TEMPLE:	Yes! He was murdered by … the Knave of Diamonds!
SIR GRAHAM:	What does your friend mean by, "But he had a sister"?
PAUL TEMPLE:	I wonder … I wonder.

The coded knocking is heard again.

DALE:	That's from the cupboard. One of the men must have come through from the house.
SIR GRAHAM:	Open the panel, Dale.

DALE slides open the panel.

DALE:	(*Annoyed*) Mowbray! What is it? I thought I told you to stay at the house!
MOWBRAY:	Sorry, sir, but this lady arrived at the house and insisted on seeing Mr Temple. I thought perhaps …
PAUL TEMPLE:	(*Surprised*) Miss Parchment!
MISS PARCHMENT:	So, we meet again, Mr Temple! How nice.

END OF EPISODE FIVE

EPISODE SIX

THE FIRST PENGUIN

Announcements. Incidental Music

PAUL TEMPLE: Interesting news, Sir Graham. It's from a friend of mine in South Africa. He's attached to the Cape Town Intelligence Department.

SIR GRAHAM: Well, what does he say?

PAUL TEMPLE: He says, "Sydney Bellman was unmarried, but he had a sister".

SIR GRAHAM: Who the devil is Sydney Bellman?

PAUL TEMPLE: He was the man who assisted Harvey when he was in South Africa. They worked together over what was known as the Simonstown Case.

SIR GRAHAM: Oh, yes, I remember. Didn't Miss Trent say he was murdered?

PAUL TEMPLE: Yes! He was murdered by … the Knave of Diamonds!

SIR GRAHAM: What does your friend mean by, "But he had a sister"?

PAUL TEMPLE: I wonder … I wonder.

The coded knocking is heard again.

DALE: That's from the cupboard. One of the men must have come through from the house.

SIR GRAHAM: Open the panel, Dale.

DALE slides open the panel.

DALE: (*Annoyed*) Mowbray! What is it? I told you to stay at the house!

MOWBRAY: Sorry, sir, but this lady arrived at the house and insisted on seeing Mr Temple. I thought perhaps …

PAUL TEMPLE: (*Surprised*) Miss Parchment!

MISS PARCHMENT: So, we meet again, Mr Temple! How nice.

119

SIR GRAHAM:	Miss Parchment! What the devil are you doing here?
MISS PARCHMENT:	Well, suppose I said, "Waiting for a bus," Sir Graham, would you believe me?
SIR GRAHAM:	Miss Parchment, this is no time for flippancy. I warn you that –
PAUL TEMPLE:	(*Interrupting*) Sir Graham, please! Miss Parchment, I know why you are here tonight. I know who you are – and what you are. But there's one question you've got to answer me … Where is Steve Trent?
MISS PARCHMENT:	Steve Trent? And who, may I ask, is Steve Trent?
PAUL TEMPLE:	Her real name is Harvey … Louise Harvey. She's the sister of Superintendent Harvey, the man who …
MISS PARCHMENT:	(*Interrupting*) Good Heavens, you don't mean Harvey … had … a sister?
PAUL TEMPLE:	Yes. And she's disappeared.
MERRITT:	Disappeared?
PAUL TEMPLE:	Yes, Charles.
DALE:	But when did this happen? Surely you didn't know anything about it when …?
PAUL TEMPLE:	(*Interrupting*) Steve's landlady arrived with the news shortly after you left for the doctor's house, Dale.
DALE:	Oh, I see.
SIR GRAHAM:	I think you'd better return to the house, Mowbray.

MOWBRAY:	Very good, sir.
DALE:	I'll come along with you. There's nothing further I can do here, Sir Graham.
SIR GRAHAM:	No. Very good, Dale.

The panel slides shut.

MISS PARCHMENT:	Mr. Temple, I should like to have a word with you. Privately, if possible.
PAUL TEMPLE:	Well … er …
SIR GRAHAM:	I, er, want to have a word with Turner, so you can come along with me, Merritt.
MERRITT:	Very good, sir.
SIR GRAHAM:	Miss Parchment, I shall want to see you later, of course.
MISS PARCHMENT:	Of course, Sir Graham.
PAUL TEMPLE:	Thank you, Sir Graham.
MERRITT:	We'll meet later, Paul.

Door closes.

MISS PARCHMENT:	(*Anxiously*) Who is that man?
PAUL TEMPLE:	Which man? Oh, Inspector Merritt. Why do you ask?
MISS PARCHMENT:	I wondered, that's all.
PAUL TEMPLE:	Well, Miss Parchment?
MISS PARCHMENT:	A little while ago, Mr Temple, you said, "I know why you are here tonight, I know who you are, and what you are" – Is that true?
PAUL TEMPLE:	Quite true.
MISS PARCHMENT:	Then tell me, and please believe me when I say this is important – do the police know … who I am?
PAUL TEMPLE:	No. No, they don't, Miss Parchment.
MISS PARCHMENT:	Ah – well, that's a relief.

PAUL TEMPLE:	Why are you so anxious to keep your identity a secret from Scotland Yard?
MISS PARCHMENT:	I think you know the answer to that question, Mr Temple.
PAUL TEMPLE:	Yes. Yes, I think perhaps I do. Miss Parchment – you've got to help me find Steve Trent.
MISS PARCHMENT:	Yes, yes, I'll help you. But first, tell me. Do you know why I am interested in old English inns?
PAUL TEMPLE:	Yes. Yes, I know. Although I must confess I was rather puzzled at first. During the last few days I have made a great many inquiries about the Cape Town-Simonstown robberies. I was very interested to learn that the Knave of Diamonds had organized and directed all his plans from a group of inns all situated in the same area. It was clever of you to assume that he would use the same in this country. You should have been a detective, Miss Parchment.
MISS PARCHMENT:	Thank you. I think the Commissioner intends to detain me on suspicion, especially after my unexpected presence here this evening. If you could persuade him to refrain from doing so, then I think the two of us might quite possibly stand a very good chance of finding Miss Trent.
PAUL TEMPLE:	Yes. I think that could be arranged.
MISS PARCHMENT:	Good. Now tell me, have you heard of "The First Penguin"?

PAUL TEMPLE:	The First Penguin? (*Pause*) Why, why yes, it's a small, deserted Inn on the river – about four miles the other side of Evesham.
MISS PARCHMENT:	That's right, Mr Temple.

Long pause.
A telephone rings and the receiver is lifted.

DIANA:	Hello! … Oh, it's you, Max … No, no they haven't … Not even Milton. I'm still waiting for them … Yes … Yes, the girl's here … I say, Max, is everything all right? … Yes … Yes, I'm listening … Saltzburg? … I see … Yes, I'll tell him … Right! Goodbye.

The telephone receiver is replaced.
Door opens.

DIANA:	You're late!
DR MILTON:	Yes, we had a hell of a game with one of the cars.
DIANA:	Where's Dixie and the others?
DR MILTON:	They should be here soon.
DIANA:	Did you get the stuff all right?
DR MILTON:	Yes. I say, what happened about that girl? Steve Trent.
DIANA:	She's here.
DR MILTON:	Here?
DIANA:	Yes.
DR MILTON:	That's a bit stupid, isn't it?
DIANA:	It was the Chief's orders to bring her back here. That's all I know.
DR MILTON:	Did you have any trouble with her?

123

DIANA: At first. We were nearly picked up in Bond Street – she screamed like mad!

DR MILTON: M'm. Heaven, I could do with a drink. No, I'll mix it.

The sound of a drink being mixed and poured.

DR MILTON: Dixie was very good tonight. He worked like a trojan.

DIANA: I'm glad you arrived first, Doc. I wanted to talk with you.

DR MILTON: Yes, I wanted to see you, too. That's why I came on ahead.

DIANA: Oh! What did you want to see me about?

DR MILTON: Can't you guess?

DIANA: No.

DR MILTON: Then I'll tell you. Six months ago, my dear Miss Thornley, you and the gentleman who prefers to call himself the Knave of Diamonds, picked me off a somewhat dilapidated tramp steamer where, partly through certain misfortunes for which I can assure you I was not to blame, I was acting as a sort of, er, shall we say, general practitioner? Indeed, not to put too fine a point on it, I was down and out!

DIANA: Well?

DR MILTON: Well, Miss Thornley – By the way, I think I'll call you Ludmilla. Miss Thornley is a trifle –

DIANA: (*Interrupting*) No one calls me Ludmilla. Except Max.

DR MILTON: Very well, then, it shall be Diana. Well, Diana, whereas six months ago I shouldn't have given a twopenny damn about what happened to me, today I find myself in the rather unique position, for me, at any rate, of looking forward to the future.

124

DIANA: I still don't understand.

DR MILTON: What I am trying to say is this. I sincerely hope that our mutual friend, the Knave of Diamonds, has no intention of depriving me of that future.

DIANA: What? Why should you think that?

DR MILTON: Oh, no particular reason. But you see, unlike Dixie and Horace, and, of course, Snow, there are times when I find myself doing quite a spot of thinking. This evening, I regret to say, was one of those occasions.

DIANA: Well?

DR MILTON: Well, Diana, oddly enough, my thoughts this evening took a rather, shall we say, creative turn of mind?

DIANA: Creative turn of mind?

DR MILTON: Yes. I wrote a letter. A long letter. Beautifully phrased and charmingly written.

DIANA: I wish to Heaven you'd talk sense!

DR MILTON: Very well, then. If, by any chance, I happen to have an unfortunate, er, accident, either now or in the near future, my beautifully phrased, charmingly written letter will be delivered straight into the hands of the Home Secretary. You will observe that I say the Home Secretary – not Scotland Yard.

DIANA: (*Anxiously*) What's in that letter?

DR MILTON: Shall we leave that to the imagination?

DIANA: You damned fool, Doc! If that letter –

DR MILTON: (*Interrupting*) That letter, I assure you, is quite safe. It will neither be posted nor opened, except, of course, in what I, at any rate, would regard as an unpleasant emergency.

DIANA: Max has no intention of double-crossing you. You've been far too valuable. He respects both your intelligence and your courage. But the others, well …

DR MILTON: What about the others?

DIANA: They've got to go.

DR MILTON: Why?

DIANA: You know perfectly well why. We're coming to the end of our rope. Things are getting a bit too hot. They've got a warrant out for every one of us, excepting the Chief. Temple overheard our meeting in Room 7 on Thursday. That's why Max switched our meeting to this place. If any one of the other three are picked up they'll talk. We can't take that chance.

DR MILTON: No, no, perhaps you're right.

DIANA: Max wants us to leave for Austria almost immediately. He'll join us later.

DR MILTON: Yes. Yes, all right. Do the boys know about the Salzburg rendezvous?

DIANA: I'm afraid so. That's what makes them so dangerous.

DR MILTON: M'm. What about the girl?

DIANA: Which girl?

DR MILTON: This girl here. Steve Trent.

DIANA: The Chief will take care of her, don't worry.

DR MILTON: Diana, why did he bring her here? What's the point?

DIANA: She's Harvey's sister.

DR MILTON: Harvey! You mean the 'tec Horace murdered at The Little General?

DIANA: Yes.

DR MILTON: I'm beginning to see daylight. Inspector Harvey had a sister … I didn't know that.

DIANA: No. And neither did the Knave until Mr Paul Temple kindly supplied the information.

DR MILTON: Paul Temple! Still got that little mess to attend to.

DIANA: Don't worry about Temple. While we've got the girl, his hands are tied.

DR MILTON: Have you heard from the Chief?

DIANA: Yes. He rang through shortly before you arrived. He wanted to know about the Malvern job.

DR MILTON: I think we might have difficulty getting some of the stuff out of the country.

DIANA: We can deal with that later. But, first of all, there's this other business …

DR MILTON: You mean – the gang …

DIANA: Yes.

DR MILTON: Leave that to me. Is – is the trapdoor working?

DIANA: Yes. And it's high tide.

DR MILTON: Good. Here, give me a hand.

The trapdoor is opened and the sound of the river below can be heard.

DIANA: Not a very pleasant part of the river, Doctor.

DR MILTON: No. But it's going to prove useful. Snow will be the first here. Horace and Dixie are coming together.

DIANA: What are you going to do?

DR MILTON: (*With a chuckle in his voice*) You'll soon see. Ah, this thing's heavy.

The trap door is closed again.

DR MILTON: That's done it.

DIANA: They know about the trapdoor, you know. It won't be a surprise.

DR MILTON: I think it will. The way I shall handle the situation. Where's that bottle of whisky?

DIANA: Here we are.

DR MILTON: Good. Now we'll each have a drink handy on the table.

The clink of glasses is heard.

DR MILTON: Good. Glasses ready for the others. That's fine. Now pass me my valise.

DIANA: What's in that small bottle?

DR MILTON: I'm going to add a little extra "kick" to the whisky, my dear, that's all. And I think our friends will find it stimulating.

DIANA: What is it?

DR MILTON: I don't think you'd be any the wiser if I told you. When Snow arrives, be drinking at all costs. He mustn't suspect anything.

DIANA: No, all right.

The sound of tyres screeching outside is heard.

DIANA: (*On edge*) What's that?

DR MILTON: It must be Snow!

DIANA: I can't see properly – this window … What –

DR MILTON: (*Interrupting*) It's Dixie!

DIANA: Isn't Horace with him?

DR MILTON: No. He must be coming with Snow later. That's funny – I was absolutely … Here he is! You know what to do.

Door opens.

DR MILTON: Hello, Dixie! I thought you were coming with Horace?

DIXIE: No. We've had a hell of a game. They must have got the alarm out pretty snappy. A cop stopped us on the outskirts of Malvern.

128

DR MILTON: (*Anxiously*) What happened?

DIXIE: Well –

DR MILTON: (*Interrupting*) You didn't …?

DIXIE: Yes. Snow let him have it!

DR MILTON: You blasted fool, Dixie!

DIXIE: It's all very well talking. We were in a jam.

DR MILTON: Why did you change cars?

DIXIE: Snow was all shot to pieces. He couldn't drive properly. I say, I feel like a drink.

DR MILTON: (*Abruptly*) What? Oh, yes! Help yourself.

DIXIE starts to pour himself a drink.

DIXIE: My God! Snow was in a state; we couldn't do anything with him.

DR MILTON: Is Horace all right?

DIXIE: Yes. I say, have you heard from the Chief?

DIANA: Yes, he's ringing again later.

DIXIE: Oh. This is the biggest job I've tackled. The safe was a devil. It was one of those –

DR MILTON: (*Interrupting*) Cheerio, Dixie!

DIXIE: Oh, cheers, Doc.

DIXIE starts to gag.

DIXIE: I say, what the hell's the matter with this … with … I say, Doc … Doc, my throat … Doc, what is it? … What is it, Doc? Oh, God I …

DR MILTON: Help me with the trap door, Diana. Quickly!

Trapdoor is opened.

DIXIE continues to writhe in pain.

DR MILTON: Right. I'll attend to him. Now, listen – go downstairs and drive his car round to the back. We don't want the others to see it when they arrive.

DIANA: Yes, all right.

Door closes.

DIXIE: (*In agony*) Doc … Doc …

129

DR MILTON: I'll take that pocketbook, my friend …

DIXIE: (*In pain*) Oh …

DR MILTON: And au revoir, Dixie!

The trap door is closed again.

DR MILTON: Whoa!

The sound of another car pulling up outside is heard.

Door opens.

DIANA: Here's Snow and Horace.

DR MILTON: Yes. I gathered that. Did they see you moving the car?

DIANA: No.

DR MILTON: You know what to do?

DIANA: Yes. Is … Is Dix–

DR MILTON: (*Interrupting*) Yes. Now be careful, we must make certain they both drink about the same time.

DIANA: Here they are!

Door opens.

DALEY: Hello, Doc.

DR MILTON: (*Cheerfully*) Hello, Horace! (*Surprised*) Where's Dixie?

DALEY: Dixie? Hasn't he arrived?

DR MILTON: No. Why – did he come on ahead?

DALEY: Yes.

DR MILTON: That's funny.

DIANA: I thought he was coming with you, Horace.

DALEY: Ah, we had a spot of bother, an' changed over. Well, here's the sparklers!

DR MILTON: Is that all the stuff?

DALEY: Yes. I think so. Blimey! Look at that diamond!

DIANA: Did you stick to the list the Chief gave you?

DALEY: He didn't give me the list. It was Dixie. I say, it's funny 'e isn't 'ere, innit?

SNOW:	Perhaps he got nervy after that spot of bother we had.
DR MILTON:	It's a pity you shot that policeman, Snow. He's almost –
SNOW:	(*Interrupting; in a panic*) I couldn't help it. I couldn't help it. He was standing there, so …
DALEY:	'Ere, just a minute! Just a minute, Doc! 'Ow did you know Snow bumped a copper off?
DR MILTON:	How did I know? Why –
DIANA:	(*Interrupting*) The Chief rang up just before you arrived. He told us.
DALEY:	Blimey! News don't 'alf travel! Why, we –
STEVE TRENT:	(*From another room*) Let me out of here! Let me out of here!
DALEY:	'Oo the 'ell is it?
DR MILTON:	It's all right. Nothing to be alarmed about. Diana, take this handkerchief; tie it tight this time. See that she can't talk.
DIANA:	Yes, all right.
Door closes.	
DALEY:	Who is it? Who's upstairs?
DR MILTON:	Steve Trent. She's a reporter with The Evening Post.
DALEY:	A reporter? What the 'ell's she doing 'ere. You've picked a ruddy good time to 'ave a reporter 'angin' abaht.
DR MILTON:	There's nothing to get alarmed about, Horace. It was the Chief's orders to bring her back here – that's all we know. What you boys want is a drink. Help yourself, Snow.
SNOW:	(*Happily*) Oh, thanks, Doc.

131

DR MILTON: Go on, Horace.

DALEY: Thanks. I don't mind if I do.

Door opens.

DIANA: Well, we shan't hear from her for a little while.

DR MILTON: The boys are having a drink, Diana.

DIANA: And they deserve it! This diamond is a whopper! Why, it must be worth a cool –

DALEY: (*Interrupting*) Blimey! I almost forgot … I got another packet outside – Dixie 'anded it to me when we switched cars. Shan't be a second.

DR MILTON: No, just a minute, Horace! You can finish your –

DALEY: Back in a jiffy, Doc.

Door closes.

SNOW: He's a hot-headed devil is 'orace!

DR MILTON: (*Quietly*) Yes.

SNOW: Well, cheerio, Doc!

DR MILTON: Ah, oh, cheerio!

SNOW: Ah! Er … er … I feel queer, Doc … It's a bit … bit … bit close in here, isn't it? Doc! Please help …!

DR MILTON: Help me with this trapdoor!

SNOW: (*In agony*) Doc! Ah! Ah!

The trapdoor is opened.

DR MILTON: That's done it!

DIANA: What about Horace?

DR MILTON: (*Straining whilst trying to move SNOW's body*) We'll look after Horace.

DIANA: Better search him!

DR MILTON: We haven't got time!

SNOW's body is thrown down into the river.

The trapdoor is closed.

DIANA: What are you going to tell Horace?

DR MILTON: I don't know. We'll tell him Snow's upstairs with the girl.

DIANA: M'm. We'd better fill Snow's glass again, or –

DR MILTON: (*Interrupting*) Here he is!

Door opens.

DALEY: Blimey! I don't know what's the matter with me. I must be imagining things. I could 'ave sworn Dixie slipped me a packet when we – 'Ello, where's Snow?

DR MILTON: He's upstairs talking to the girl.

DALEY: Oo the 'ell does 'e think 'e is? Ivor Novella?

DR MILTON: (*Chuckling nervously*) He'll be down in a minute. Here's your drink, Horace.

DALEY: Oh, thanks.

DR MILTON: Cheerio!

DALEY: Cheerio, Doc.

DR MILTON: Why don't you drink?

DALEY: I'm thinking of the copper. I 'ope to Gawd Snow did 'im in proper. 'E 'ad a good decko at us.

DR MILTON: You're nervy, Horace. What you want is a good, stiff drink.

DALEY: Yeah, perhaps you're right, Doc.

A pause.

DR MILTON: (*Anxiously*) What is it, Horace?

DALEY: I'm listening, that's all. Can't 'ear voices.

DR MILTON: Why should you hear voices?

DALEY: Why, Snow, o' course. You said he was upstairs.

DR MILTON: (*Jovially*) Well, perhaps he's not talking just now.

DALEY: Then what the 'ell is 'e doing?

133

DIANA: (*Laughs*) You certainly are jumpy, Horace.

DR MILTON: For a man who's just made the best part of a cool five thousand, you don't seem very bright, Horace.

DALEY: (*Surprised*) Five thousand?

DR MILTON: That's right. That's going to be your cut of the Malvern job, isn't it, Diana?

DIANA: That's what the Chief said.

DALEY: Five thousand smackers! Cor! That's what I call money!

DR MILTON: It's what we all call money, Horace.

DALEY: (*Delighted; laughing*) Blimey! Will I paint the town red!

They all laugh together.

DR MILTON: Well, here's luck!

DALEY: Thank you, Doc.

DIANA: Drink up, Horace.

DALEY: (*A pause*) Five … thousand! Cor, fair takes your breath away, doesn't it, Doc?

DR MILTON: It certainly seems to have taken your breath away. What the devil's the matter with you, Horace? Are you on the wagon?

DALEY: On what wagon?

DIANA: Yes, you're not drinking, Horace.

DALEY: Oh! On the wagon! (*Laughing*) Can you imagine it, Doc? Me – on the wagon, eh? Me on the wagon! That's good! That's good!

DIANA: (*Laughing heartily*) Horace on the wagon! That's certainly funny!

DALEY: I was only on it once, Doc. But I couldn't see straight.

They all laugh loudly.

DIANA: Well, cheerio!

DR MILTON: Cheerio, Diana! Drink up, Horace!

A long pause.

DR MILTON: (*Coldly*) Why aren't you drinking?

DALEY: Because I'm not a prize sucker, Doc. Stand away from that door!

DR MILTON: Put that gun down, Horace. Don't be a damn fool!

DALEY: Stand away from that door, or I'll blow your blasted brains out! Drink up, Horace! Are you on the wagon, Horace? Cheerio, Horace! (*Laughing sinisterly*) 'Ere, take this glass, Doc! Take it!

DR MILTON: No! No!

DALEY: What have you done with Dixie and Snow?

DR MILTON: I tell you, we haven't seen Dixie!

DALEY: Don't tell your blarsted lies! His car's at the back!

DR MILTON: (*Urgently*) Now, listen, Horace, if you take my –

DALEY: I'm taking nothing from you or anybody else from now on, Doc. I'm giving the orders, see! Now drink this!

DR MILTON: No! No!

DALEY: Drink it!

DIANA: Here! I'll drink it.

DALEY: You!

DIANA: Yes. There's nothing in the glass except whisky. Come, give me the glass and I'll prove it!

DALEY: All right! All right, Miss Clever! If that's how you feel about it – Here we are.

DIANA: Thank you. Well, cheerio, Doc.

DIANA throws the drink into DALEY's face.

DALEY: (*Writhing in pain*) Oh, my face! My face! Oh, my God, my face …

135

DALEY's body falls to the ground.

DR MILTON: Smart girl!

DIANA: What did you hit him with?

DR MILTON: This revolver. I had it in my hand all the time, but I was frightened to shoot.

DIANA: He's not dead.

DR MILTON: No, but we'll soon –

A car is heard pulling up outside.

DR MILTON: What's that?

DIANA: It's a car!

DR MILTON: Who the devil can that be?

DIANA: I can't see very clearly. The window … Why, it's that woman … Miss Parchment.

DR MILTON: Miss Parchment! Is she alone?

DIANA: Yes. As far as I can see.

DR MILTON: Open that cupboard door! We'll push Horace in there!

DIANA: What about the river? Can't you –

DR MILTON: (*Interrupting*) No. We haven't time. (*Struggling to move the body*) It's all right. It'll be a hell of a time before he comes round. Can you still see that old dame?

DIANA: Yes. She's coming into the Inn. I say, Doc. Who the devil is this woman?

DR MILTON: Don't ask me!

DIANA: She seems to be turning up all over the place.

Cupboard door is closed.

DIANA: First she was at The Little General. Then she was at the Yard when Skid was bumped off, and now she's –

DR MILTON: (*Interrupting*) I reckon she's a 'tec.

DIANA: Then what's she doing here?

DR MILTON: Probably trying to find that girl. Steve Trent.

DIANA:	M'm. Well, she's got a nerve; I'll say that for her.
DR MILTON:	She's coming through the bar parlour. Stand away from the door.
DIANA:	All right.

Door opens.

DR MILTON:	Good evening, Miss Parchment!
MISS PARCHMENT:	Why, Dr Milton! How very nice!
DR MILTON:	Come in here, and drop that handbag! Drop it!
MISS PARCHMENT:	Very well.
DR MILTON:	Pick it up, Diana.
DIANA:	Okay.

Door closes.

MISS PARCHMENT:	I do hope that gun isn't loaded, Doctor. Your hand is quite shaky, and …
DR MILTON:	(*Interrupting*) Miss Parchment … what are you doing here … at The First Penguin?
MISS PARCHMENT:	Well, really, Doctor, your tone of voice!
DR MILTON:	Miss Parchment! Answer my question!
MISS PARCHMENT:	I – I came to see a friend.
DR MILTON:	Which friend?
MISS PARCHMENT:	A Miss Trent. A Miss Steve Trent. Now don't tell me you've never heard of her.
DIANA:	How did you know Steve Trent was here?
MISS PARCHMENT:	How did I know? A bird told me, Miss Thornley. Not a little bird. Shall we say … a pigeon?

DIANA:	Doc! She's only stalling for time. There's something in the wind!

Door opens suddenly.

PAUL TEMPLE:	Drop that gun, Milton!
DR MILTON:	Temple!
DIANA:	(*Angrily*) How the devil did you get here?
PAUL TEMPLE:	I came with Miss Parchment. I regret not having joined you earlier, but I had a little difficulty in locating Miss Trent. Steve! Take his gun!
STEVE TRENT:	All right, Paul.
PAUL TEMPLE:	Would you mind sitting over there, Miss Thornley? Thank you. Hold this gun, Miss Parchment. If either of them moves while Miss Trent and I are making them comfortable, well, you know what to do.
MISS PARCHMENT:	Oh, er, er, rather, Mr Temple.
STEVE TRENT:	Here's the rope, Paul.
PAUL TEMPLE:	Thanks. Now for a dose of your own medicine, my friends!
MISS PARCHMENT:	What's all this jewellery on the table?
PAUL TEMPLE:	It's from the Malvern job, unless I'm very much mistaken.
STEVE TRENT:	Yes. Horace Daley and two other men arrived with it. I could hear them talking … Suddenly they seemed to disappear … I could hear some sort of a trapdoor being opened … and then what sounded to me like a splash of some sort … I had a feeling –

PAUL TEMPLE:	Oh! Oh, that's interesting. So you've been getting rid of the small fry, eh, Doc?
DR MILTON:	I'll get you for this, Temple! I'll get you if it takes twenty years!
PAUL TEMPLE:	(*Unbothered*) H'm. Yes, here's the trapdoor all right.

PAUL opens the trapdoor.

| PAUL TEMPLE: | By Timothy, Steve! The river! |

The trapdoor is closed again.

MISS PARCHMENT:	Mr Temple, would you relieve me of this revolver? I always feel that it …
PAUL TEMPLE:	(*Pleasantly*) Yes, of course. There's no necessity for it anyhow, now that our delightful friends are tied up. Steve, how many people arrived here tonight?
STEVE TRENT:	Three. Horace Daley; the man who admitted us to Ashdown House that time; and the other man we heard in Room 7. I think his name was Dixie.
PAUL TEMPLE:	H'm h'm.
STEVE TRENT:	The doctor was the first to arrive; he came alone.
PAUL TEMPLE:	I see.
STEVE TRENT:	Just before the doctor came, I heard the telephone. It was Max Lorraine. I could only just hear what Diana Thornley was saying –
DIANA:	(*Interrupting*) She's lying! She's lying! She's lying, I tell you.
STEVE TRENT:	They were obviously planning a get-away. I heard the girl mention

	Saltzburg. When the doctor arrived, she said the Knave would ring later.
PAUL TEMPLE:	Later! By Timothy, if he rings again, we might trace the call!
DIANA:	I tell you, she's lying! She's lying!
DR MILTON:	You blasted fool, Temple! You don't really think that –

The telephone begins to ring.

| STEVE TRENT: | That's … that's him! |
| PAUL TEMPLE: | Yes. I'll answer it. |

PAUL lifts the telephone receiver.

PAUL TEMPLE:	(*Calmly; on phone*) Hello … Hello.
STEVE TRENT:	What's happened?
PAUL TEMPLE:	He's rung off.
STEVE TRENT:	Did you recognise the voice?
PAUL TEMPLE:	No. But we'll trace the call.

PAUL taps on the telephone.

PAUL TEMPLE:	(*On phone*) Hello! Is that the Exchange? This is Paul Tempe speaking … I'm speaking for Sir Graham Forbes, Chief Commissioner of Police … I've just received a telephone call and I want you to trace it for me … Yes … Yes, just this minute … It's very urgent … The number is, er, Evesham 9986 … Yes, all right.
STEVE TRENT:	Is she tracing it?
PAUL TEMPLE:	Yes. (*Pause*) Hello? Yes! … Yes! … What! … What! … I see … Thank you.
MISS PARCHMENT:	Well, Mr Temple?
STEVE TRENT:	Where did the call come from?
PAUL TEMPLE:	It came from my own house, Steve.

STEVE TRENT: From Bramley Lodge?
PAUL TEMPLE: (*Quietly*) Yes. From Bramley Lodge.
DR MILTON laughs.

END OF EPISODE SIX

EPISODE SEVEN

THE KNAVE OF DIAMONDS

Announcements. Incidental music.

DR MILTON: Cheerio, Diana! Drink up, Horace!

A long pause.

DR MILTON: (*Coldly*) Why aren't you drinking?

DALEY: Because I'm not a prize sucker, Doc. Stand away from that door!

DR MILTON: Put that gun down, Horace. Don't be a damn fool!

DALEY: Stand away from that door, or I'll blow your blasted brains out! Drink up, Horace! Are you on the wagon, Horace? Cheerio, Horace! (*Laughing sinisterly*) 'Ere, take this glass, Doc! Take it!

DR MILTON: No! No!

DALEY: What have you done with Dixie and Snow?

DR MILTON: I tell you, we haven't seen Dixie!

DALEY: Don't tell your blarsted lies! His car's at the back!

DR MILTON: (*Urgently*) Now, listen, Horace, if you take my –

DALEY: I'm taking nothing from you or anybody else from now on. Doc. I'm giving the orders, see! Now drink this!

DR MILTON: No! No!

DALEY: Drink it!

DIANA: Here! I'll drink it.

DALEY: You!

DIANA: Yes. There's nothing in the glass except whisky. Come, give me the glass and I'll prove it!

DALEY: All right! All right, Miss Clever! If that's how you feel about it – Here we are.

DIANA: Thank you. Well, cheerio, Doc.

145

DIANA throws the drink into DALEY's face.

DALEY: (*Writhing in pain*) Oh, my face! My face! Oh, my God, my face …

DALEY's body falls to the ground.

DR MILTON: Smart girl!

DIANA: What did you hit him with?

DR MILTON: This revolver. I had it in my hand all the time, but I was frightened to shoot.

DIANA: He's not dead.

DR MILTON: No, but we'll soon –

A car is heard pulling up outside.

DR MILTON: What's that?

DIANA: It's a car!

DR MILTON: Who the devil can that be?

DIANA: I can't see very clearly. The window … Why, why it's that woman … Miss Parchment.

DR MILTON: Miss Parchment! Is she alone?

DIANA: Yes. As far as I can see.

DR MILTON: Open that cupboard door! We'll push Horace in there!

DIANA: What about the river? Can't you –

DR MILTON: (*Interrupting*) No. We haven't time. (*Struggling to move the body*) It's all right. It'll be a hell of a time before he comes round. Can you still see that old dame?

DIANA: Yes. She's coming into the Inn. I say, Doc. Who the devil is this woman?

DR MILTON: Don't ask me!

DIANA: She seems to be turning up all over the place.

Cupboard door is closed.

DIANA: First she was at The Little General. Then she was at the Yard when Skid was bumped off, and now she's –

DR MILTON: (*Interrupting*) I reckon she's a 'tec.

DIANA:	Then what's she doing here?
DR MILTON:	Probably trying to find that girl. Steve Trent.
DIANA:	M'm. Well, she's got a nerve; I'll say that for her.
DR MILTON:	She's coming through the bar parlour. Stand away from the door.
DIANA:	All right.
Door opens.	
DR MILTON:	Good evening, Miss Parchment!
MISS PARCHMENT:	Why, Dr Milton! How very nice!
DR MILTON:	Come in here, and drop that handbag! Drop it!
MISS PARCHMENT:	Very well.
DR MILTON:	Pick it up, Diana.
DIANA:	Okay.
Door closes.	
MISS PARCHMENT:	I do hope that gun isn't loaded, Doctor. You hand is quite shaky, and …
DR MILTON:	(*Interrupting*) Miss Parchment … what are you doing here … at The First Penguin?
MISS PARCHMENT:	Well, really, Doctor, your tone of voice!
DR MILTON:	Miss Parchment! Answer my question!
MISS PARCHMENT:	I – I came to see a friend.
DR MILTON:	Which friend?
MISS PARCHMENT:	A Miss Trent. A Miss Steve Trent. Now don't tell me you've never heard of her.
DIANA:	How did you know Steve Trent was here?

MISS PARCHMENT:	How did I know? A bird told me, Miss Thornley. Not a little bird. Shall we say … a pigeon?
DIANA:	Doc! She's only stalling for time. There's something in the wind!

Door opens suddenly.

PAUL TEMPLE:	Drop that gun, Milton!
DR MILTON:	Temple!
DIANA:	(*Angrily*) How the devil did you get here?
PAUL TEMPLE:	I came with Miss Parchment. I regret not having joined you earlier, but I had a little difficulty in locating Miss Trent. Steve! Take his gun!
STEVE TRENT:	All right, Paul.
PAUL TEMPLE:	Would you mind sitting over there, Miss Thornley? Thank you. Hold this gun, Miss Parchment. If either of them moves while Miss Trent and I are making them comfortable, well, you know what to do.
MISS PARCHMENT:	Oh, er, er, rather, Mr Temple.
STEVE TRENT:	Here's the rope, Paul.
PAUL TEMPLE:	Thanks. Now for a dose of your own medicine, my friends!
MISS PARCHMENT:	What's all this jewellery on the table?
PAUL TEMPLE:	It's from the Malvern job, unless I'm very much mistaken.
STEVE TRENT:	Yes. Horace Daley and two other men arrived with it. I could hear them talking … Suddenly they seemed to disappear … I could hear some sort of a trapdoor being opened … and then

what sounded to me like a splash of some sort … I had a feeling –

PAUL TEMPLE: Oh! Oh, that's interesting. So you've been getting rid of the small fry, eh, Doc?

DR MILTON: I'll get you for this, Temple! I'll get you if it takes twenty years!

PAUL TEMPLE: (*Unbothered*) H'm h'm. Yes, here's the trapdoor all right.

PAUL opens the trapdoor and the sound of the river can be heard.

PAUL TEMPLE: By Timothy, Steve! The river!

The trapdoor is closed again.

MISS PARCHMENT: Mr Temple, would you relieve me of this revolver? I always feel that it …

PAUL TEMPLE: (*Pleasantly*) Yes, of course. There's no necessity for it anyhow, now that our delightful friends are tied up. Steve, how many people arrived here tonight?

STEVE TRENT: Three. Horace Daley; the man who admitted us to Ashdown House that time; and the other man we heard in Room 7. I think his name was Dixie.

PAUL TEMPLE: H'm h'm.

STEVE TRENT: The doctor was the first to arrive; he came alone.

PAUL TEMPLE: I see.

STEVE TRENT: Just before the doctor came, I heard the telephone. It was Max Lorraine. I could only just hear what Diana Thornley was saying –

DIANA: (*Interrupting*) She's lying! She's lying! She's lying, I tell you.

149

STEVE TRENT:	They were obviously planning a get-away. I heard the girl mention Saltzburg. When the doctor arrived, she said the Knave would ring later.
PAUL TEMPLE:	Later! By Timothy, if he rings again, we might trace the call!
DIANA:	I tell you, she's lying! She's lying!
DR MILTON:	You blasted fool, Temple! You don't really think that –

The telephone begins to ring.

| STEVE TRENT: | That's … that's him! |
| PAUL TEMPLE: | Yes. I'll answer it. |

PAUL lifts the telephone receiver.

PAUL TEMPLE:	(*Calmly; on phone*) Hello … Hello.
STEVE TRENT:	What's happened?
PAUL TEMPLE:	He's rung off.
STEVE TRENT:	Did you recognise the voice?
PAUL TEMPLE:	No. But we'll trace the call.

PAUL taps on the telephone.

PAUL TEMPLE:	(*On phone*) Hello! Is that the Exchange? This is Paul Tempe speaking … I'm speaking for Sir Graham Forbes, Chief Commissioner of Police … I've just received a telephone call and I want you to trace it … Yes … Yes, just this minute … It's very urgent … The number is, er, Evesham 9986 … Yes, all right.
STEVE TRENT:	Is she tracing it?
PAUL TEMPLE:	Yes. (*Pause*) Hello? Yes! … Yes! … What! … What! … I see … Thank you.
MISS PARCHMENT:	Well, Mr Temple?
STEVE TRENT:	Where did the call come from?

PAUL TEMPLE:	It came from my own house, Steve.
STEVE TRENT:	From Bramley Lodge?
PAUL TEMPLE:	(*Quietly*) Yes. From Bramley Lodge.

DR MILTON laughs.

| STEVE TRENT: | Hadn't you better – |
| PAUL TEMPLE: | (*Interrupting*) I'll get on to Pryce to see who's at the house. |

PAUL lifts the telephone receiver.

PAUL TEMPLE:	(*On phone*) Hello, miss, will you get me Evesham 9898? … Yes, thank you.
STEVE TRENT:	Paul –
PAUL TEMPLE:	Yes?
STEVE TRENT:	Oh, I know this sounds silly, but … How long has Pryce been working for you?
PAUL TEMPLE:	You don't have to worry about Pryce, Steve. He isn't the Knave of Diamonds, I assure you. He looks far too guilty after snaffling one of my cigars – or perhaps it's the cigars! (*On phone*) Hello? … Yes, miss … What? … Oh, but there must be … Out of order? … Oh … Oh, I see. Thank you.

PAUL replaces the telephone receiver.

| STEVE TRENT: | What's the matter? |
| PAUL TEMPLE: | There's no reply. Or rather they can't get the number … There's something funny, Steve. Look here, we must get back to Bramley Lodge as quickly as we can. |

STEVE TRENT:	Paul, the Knave must be someone you know fairly well – otherwise Pryce wouldn't have admitted him.
PAUL TEMPLE:	Yes, of course. H'm. Miss Parchment, you stay here with Milton and the girl. It's imperative that I get back to Bramley Lodge as quickly as possible. If the Knave has been there, and he obviously has, then this is the chance we've been waiting for.
MISS PARCHMENT:	Yes. Yes, all right, Mr Temple.
PAUL TEMPLE:	Take this revolver. If they try any funny business – use it.
DIANA:	You can't leave us here – tied up like this!
DR MILTON:	Listen, Temple, if you think –
PAUL TEMPLE:	(*Interrupting*) I'll get Sir Graham to send someone here immediately I get back to the house.
MISS PARCHMENT:	That's all right, Mr Temple. I shall be quite comfortable.
PAUL TEMPLE:	Good. We'd better take these diamonds. Have you got a handbag, Steve?
STEVE TRENT:	Yes.
PAUL TEMPLE:	Ah, splendid!

The diamonds are put into STEVE's bag.

PAUL TEMPLE:	See you later, Miss Parchment.
MISS PARCHMENT:	Yes. Goodbye.

Door closes.

Incidental Music plays.
A car door is opened.

PAUL TEMPLE:	Jump in!

152

STEVE TRENT: How long should it take us?

PAUL TEMPLE: About twenty minutes. With a bit of luck we – we should …

STEVE TRENT: Paul! What is it?

PAUL TEMPLE: I say, did you see that pigeon?

STEVE TRENT: Why, yes! There's a courtyard at the back full of them.

PAUL TEMPLE: How do you know?

STEVE TRENT: Because I could see them from the room I was in.

PAUL TEMPLE: Good Lord! Why on earth didn't I think of it?

STEVE TRENT: Paul! What's the matter?

PAUL TEMPLE: Do you remember? The Constable commented on the pigeons at The Little General.

STEVE TRENT: Well?

PAUL TEMPLE: Steve! Steve, wait here … I shan't be a second … Start the car!

STEVE starts the car and the engine ticks over.

STEVE TRENT: Well, what's all the mystery about?

PAUL TEMPLE: Sorry to dash off like that, but there was something I rather wanted to check up on.

STEVE TRENT: And did you?

PAUL TEMPLE: Yes. I checked up on it –

STEVE TRENT: (*Giggles*) Of all the tantalising … Paul! Paul! I've just thought – They're – they're carrier pigeons!

PAUL TEMPLE: Yes. They're carrier pigeons all right! And now for Bramley Lodge and the Knave of Diamonds!

Incidental Music.

DR MILTON: (*Fade in*) Miss Parchment, if you don't …

153

MISS PARCHMENT:	Dear Dr Milton, if I've told you once, I've told you a hundred times. There is absolutely nothing to be gained by these, er, primitive outbursts. You're staying in that chair until Mr Temple returns, and if there's any funny business, I shall press this trigger. I shall press this trigger, Dr Milton!
DR MILTON:	My God! When I get out of this …
DIANA:	Shut up, Doc! Shut up! There's nothing to be gained by kicking up a row! We're in a jam and we've got to make the best of it.
MISS PARCHMENT:	Ah, you have a philosophical side to your character, Miss Thornley – I congratulate you.
DIANA:	Miss Parchment, I've come up against a great many people in my time, and a great many – shall we say – awkward situations. But, well, you're – you're sort of different. How do you fit into all this?
MISS PARCHMENT:	So you're puzzled, Miss Thornley?
DIANA:	Yes … I'm puzzled. And so are a great many other people, for that matter. Even the Knave can't figure you out. And he isn't often puzzled by people – or situations.
MISS PARCHMENT:	Yes, Yes, I can quite believe that.
DIANA:	First of all, you turned up at The Little General. By some means or other you discovered that it was called The Green Finger and that it was the headquarters of our

	organisation. How did you discover that?
MISS PARCHMENT:	I made it my purpose to find out, Miss Thornley. I became interested in old English Inns.
DIANA:	Yes. But why?
MISS PARCHMENT:	Because I was pretty certain that the Knave would direct his activities in much the same way as he did in Cape Town – from a group of inns all situated in the same area.
DIANA:	(*Surprised; urgently*) How did you know that? How did you know the Knave was in Cape Town?
MISS PARCHMENT:	The Little General was an obvious choice. It had been for sale quite a little while. And then there was the passage from Ashdown House ... I heard about that quite by accident, while trying to gather information about this place.
DIANA:	(*Anxiously*) Miss Parchment, you haven't answered my question. How did you know the Knave was ever in Cape Town?
MISS PARCHMENT:	Do you remember a man on the Cape Town Constabulary called Bellman, Sydney Bellman?
DIANA:	Why ... why, yes ...
MISS PARCHMENT:	The Knave murdered him!
DIANA:	Why are you looking like that?
DR MILTON:	Good God, she's shaking! Put that gun down or it will go off! Miss Parchment, put that gun down.

MISS PARCHMENT: Sydney Bellman was my brother!

DIANA: (*Surprised*) Your … brother …!

MISS PARCHMENT: Yes. And now, my dear Miss Thornley, my dear Dr Milton, I am going to give you exactly thirty seconds to tell me – Who is the Knave?

DR MILTON: (*Frightened*) All right! All right! But put that gun down …

DIANA: Keep your mouth shut, you swine! If you so much as –

There is an unexpected noise behind Miss Parchment.

MISS PARCHMENT: What's that?

DIANA: Look out, Horace! Look out!

The gun goes off.

DR MILTON: She's missed him!

There are the sounds of a tussle.

DIANA: Good, Horace! Good!

DALEY: I don't know what the 'ell you're doing here, but get into that cupboard. Get into that cupboard!

MISS PARCHMENT: Mr Daley! Mr Daley! I must ask you –

DALEY: (*Interrupting*) Get into that cupboard or –

Cupboard door is closed.

DR MILTON: Get us untied. Horace, quickly!

DALEY: Strewth! My 'ead is like a blasted furnace.

DIANA: Horace – untie us – quickly!

DALEY: What? Oh no, no, you don't! So, where's the stuff?

156

DR MILTON: Horace, for God's sake! Don't stand there! Get this rope untied. We must get out of here.

DIANA: Quickly, Horace!

DALEY: Listen, you two, where's the stuff?

DR MILTON: Get the rope free, Horace, and then –

DALEY: (*Angrily*) I'm asking – who's got the stuff? Who's got the diamonds?

DR MILTON: Horace … we've got to get out of here. (*Desperate*) We've got to! No, no, Horace! No! Horace!

DALEY: Now listen, Doc, if you don't tell me where the stuff is, I'll break every bone in your blasted –

DR MILTON: No, no! All right! Temple's got it. He left about ten minutes ago with the girl –

DIANA: Horace! Where are you going?

DALEY: To get the stuff back!

DR MILTON: You've got to untie us first!

DALEY: That's your guess, Doc!

DIANA: Horace, listen! Temple's gone after the Knave – he traced a telephone call – you've got to set us free! You've got to –

DALEY: To hell with the Knave!

DIANA: (*Desperately*) Horace, you've got to get us out of here … You've got to!

DR MILTON: For Heaven's sake, Horace … listen … we must tell …

DALEY: Temple's got the diamonds! Right! That's all I want to know!

Door slams shut.

DIANA: Horace! Horace!

DR MILTON: The dirty, double-crossing little swine! When I get out of here, I'll –

A commotion is heard coming from inside the cupboard.

MISS PARCHMENT: (*From inside the cupboard*) Let me
out! Let me out!

Incidental music.

The sound of a car engine turning.

STEVE TRENT: How far have we got to go now, Paul?

PAUL TEMPLE: Not very far. About two miles. Steve …
you haven't told me what happened? How
you came to be at The First Penguin.

STEVE TRENT: Well, there's nothing much to say, really.
Early this morning, I received a telephone
call which was supposed to be from the
paper. They said they wanted to see me
immediately. It sounded quite genuine –
but when I got outside the flat, I noticed a
saloon car. It was drawn up close to the
kerb. A girl got out of the car and came
across to me. I forget now what she said
… but before I could do anything, a man
came up from behind … took me by the
arm … and well, the next thing I knew
was that I was sitting in the back of the
car.

PAUL TEMPLE: Well, thank God Miss Parchment knew
about The First Penguin.

STEVE TRENT: Paul, who is Miss Parchment?

PAUL TEMPLE: Her name is Bellman. Amelia Bellman.
She's the sister to the man who helped
your brother over the Cape Town
robberies.

STEVE TRENT: Sydney Bellman! But – he was murdered –
by – Max Lorraine!

PAUL TEMPLE: Yes, and from the very moment he was
murdered, Miss Parchment made up her

158

mind to track down the Knave. She knew quite a lot about the way Lorraine worked. In fact, if the Knave had known who Miss Parchment was, then, believe me, he wouldn't have wasted his time in kidnapping Louise Harvey.

STEVE TRENT: Does Miss Parchment know who the Knave really is?

PAUL TEMPLE: No. No, she doesn't. But I think she's got a pretty shrewd idea. We raided The Little General tonight, but the place was deserted. Except for Miss Parchment.

STEVE TRENT: What was she doing there?

PAUL TEMPLE: Apparently she'd read somewhere or other there was a passage between Ashdown House and The Little General, and she chose tonight, of all nights, to investigate the fact.

STEVE TRENT: It's perhaps a good job she did. Or I might still have been at The First Penguin – waiting for … Max Lorraine …

PAUL TEMPLE: Steve, you don't know how glad I felt when I broke into that room and saw you there. All the way down to the Inn, I was … I was hoping to God you'd be safe.

STEVE TRENT: Well, believe me, Paul, the relief wasn't one-sided.

PAUL TEMPLE: It's rather funny about Miss Parchment. I tumbled to her identity after we'd visited Ashdown House. You remember I asked you the name of the man who assisted your brother in Cape Town … At first, I had a feeling that Miss Parchment might have been his wife.

STEVE TRENT:	Does Sir Graham know about Miss Parchment?
PAUL TEMPLE:	No, I don't think so. I'm afraid there are one or two surprises on hand for Sir Graham. And you'll be one of them, Steve, unless I'm very much mistaken.
STEVE TRENT:	What do you mean?
PAUL TEMPLE:	Well, when I left The Little General, I told him I was taking Miss Parchment back to Bramley Lodge. He'll get rather a shock to find we've visited an outlandish Inn known at The First Penguin, captured the doctor and Diana Thornley, recovered the proceeds of the Malvern robbery, and rescued you into the bargain.
STEVE TRENT:	(*Chuckles*) Yes. Yes, I suppose he will. Paul, why didn't you tell Sir Graham you were going with Miss Parchment to The First Penguin?
PAUL TEMPLE:	I don't think that would have been too wise, Steve. In more senses than one.
STEVE TRENT:	Why do you say that?
PAUL TEMPLE:	When Skid Tyler was murdered it was in Sir Graham's office at Scotland Yard. When Sir Graham and I devised a little plan about an imaginary "Trenchman" diamond, the Knave got to know about it. When we decided to raid The Little General tonight, the Inn was deserted.
STEVE TRENT:	Paul – Paul, you don't think Sir Graham is … the Knave?
PAUL TEMPLE:	I don't know who the Knave is, Steve, but I know that he has been to Bramley Lodge

tonight, and when we – I say, that car's coming up rather quickly, isn't it?

STEVE TRENT: Paul! It's one of the cars from the Inn!

PAUL TEMPLE: But it can't be!

STEVE TRENT: It is! It's the red one that – Paul, it's Horace Daley!

PAUL TEMPLE: Daley!

STEVE TRENT: He's recognized us! Paul! He's got a gun! He's – look out, Paul! Look out!

The sound of the windscreen shattering is heard.

PAUL TEMPLE: (*Urgently*) Steve! Are you all right?

STEVE TRENT: Yes. He hit the window at the back.

PAUL TEMPLE: Keep down!

STEVE TRENT: Paul, he's going to pass you!

PAUL TEMPLE: No. We mustn't let him do that. Steve, listen! There's a bridge round the next bend. As soon as we reach it, I'll slow down and let him overtake us. Then we'll force him over the top. It's our only chance!

STEVE TRENT: Yes, yes, all right!

PAUL TEMPLE: Wrap the rug round your head and keep down!

STEVE TRENT: Look out!

The front windscreen shatters.

PAUL TEMPLE: It's only the windscreen! Keep down!

STEVE TRENT: Paul! You're hurt!

PAUL TEMPLE: No … no, I'm all right.

The sound of the two cars chasing each other.

PAUL TEMPLE: Here's the bridge! Now keep down!

STEVE TRENT: He's passing us, Paul! Look out, he's forcing you over! He's –

PAUL TEMPLE: Hold on, Steve!

161

The sound of the two cars colliding and then DALEY's car crashing into the bridge wall and falling into the water below.

PAUL TEMPLE: Steve, are you all right?

STEVE TRENT: Yes. Yes, I'm all right. Paul, you're hurt!

PAUL TEMPLE: No. No, it's nothing. It's only a scratch. I say, we'd better get out of here. The car's half over the bridge.

The sound of a car part falling off.

PAUL TEMPLE: Careful, Steve … careful.

STEVE TRENT: Paul, look! There's Horace! He's on the side! He must have been thrown out of the car against the wall!

PAUL TEMPLE: Yes. Yes. He's in a pretty bad way. Wait here, Steve.

The sound of footsteps.

DALEY is groaning.

DALEY: I – I'm sorry, Guv'nor. Honest. I am – I only – Oh, oh …

PAUL TEMPLE: Horace, listen. (*Slowly*) Who is the Knave?

DALEY: Oh …

PAUL TEMPLE: Horace. Horace?

STEVE TRENT: How – how is he?

PAUL TEMPLE: He's – he's dead. (*Pause; sombrely*) We'll have to walk into the village, Steve. It's about half a mile, I think.

Pause.

Door closes.

PRYCE: Well, this _is_ a surprise, sir!

PAUL TEMPLE: Pryce, listen! Has anyone been here tonight, since I left with Sir Graham for The Little General?

PRYCE: Why, yes, sir. Inspector Merritt –

PAUL TEMPLE: (*Interrupting; urgently*) Inspector Merritt?

162

PRYCE:	Yes, sir. He's downstairs with Inspector Dale and Sir Graham. They're waiting for you in the drawing-room, sir. Shall I tell them that you've arrived?
PAUL TEMPLE:	No! I don't want them to know I'm here; that's why I came in through the back entrance.
PRYCE:	I – I see, sir.
PAUL TEMPLE:	Pryce, now tell me. How long has Sir Graham been here?
PRYCE:	About, er, two hours, sir. He rather expected to find you here, sir, when he arrived.
PAUL TEMPLE:	What did he say?
PRYCE:	He asked me if I'd seen you, sir – or a Miss Parchment. I told him that you had not been here since, er, yourself and Sir Graham left for The Little General.
PAUL TEMPLE:	H'm. Was he alone?
PRYCE:	No, sir. Inspector Merritt was with him.
PAUL TEMPLE:	Inspector Merritt … Oh, I see. Well, when did Dale arrive?
PRYCE:	Much later than the others, sir. He came from Ashdown House, I believe.
PAUL TEMPLE:	Yes. Now, Pryce, tell me, then what happened?
PRYCE:	Then I believe Inspector Dale and Sir Graham went back to the Inn, sir. The Little General.
PAUL TEMPLE:	Leaving Inspector Merritt here?
PRYCE:	Yes, sir.
PAUL TEMPLE:	In the drawing-room, I presume?
PRYCE:	Yes, sir. In the drawing-room.

PAUL TEMPLE: Did Inspector Merritt use the telephone, do you know, Pryce?

PRYCE: Yes, I believe he did, now you come to mention it. I was passing through the hall and I heard the bell … You know how it tinkles, sir.

PAUL TEMPLE: Yes. Then I expect Sir Graham and Dale returned from the Inn?

PRYCE: Yes, sir, and almost immediately two of them departed for Ashdown House again.

PAUL TEMPLE: Which two? Merritt and Dale, or –

PRYCE: That I couldn't say, sir. I was in the kitchen getting Mrs Neddy a cup of tea. I heard voices in the hall and then the front door slammed.

PAUL TEMPLE: What time would that be – about 10.30?

PRYCE: Yes, sir. A little later, if anything, sir.

PAUL TEMPLE: H'm.

PRYCE: After a short while they returned from Ashdown House, sir, and all three of them – Sir Graham Forbes, Inspector Dale, and Inspector Merritt – have all been in the drawing-room ever since.

PAUL TEMPLE: H'm. Is there any ink in here, and writing paper?

PRYCE: Er, why yes, sir. It's on the desk.

PAUL TEMPLE: Good. Now, Pryce, listen. I'm going to write a short note. While I'm writing it, you slip round to the garage, get the small car out, and take it to the end of the drive. Miss Trent is there waiting. She'll take over. Is that clear?

PRYCE: Yes, sir.

164

PAUL TEMPLE:	Now, Pryce, this is important. Under no circumstances must Sir Graham, Inspector Dale, or Inspector Merritt know that I have been here! Is that understood?
PRYCE:	Yes, sir.
PAUL TEMPLE:	Good! Now, where's this writing paper? Oh, here we are! Do you know, Pryce, I think this is probably going to be my greatest contribution to popular fiction! Yes, by Timothy, I'm sure it is.

Incidental music.

A car engine turning over can be heard.

PRYCE:	Miss Trent! Miss Trent.
STEVE TRENT:	Oh, here you are, Pryce. Good.
PRYCE:	Mr Temple said you would take over from here, Miss –
STEVE TRENT:	(*Interrupting*) Yes, that's all right, Pryce.
PRYCE:	Here is Mr Temple.
PAUL TEMPLE:	Ah, you've got the car. Good! Now get back to the house, Pryce, and remember what I told you.
PRYCE:	Yes, sir. Good night, miss. Good night, sir.
PAUL TEMPLE:	Merritt, Dale, and Sir Graham are at the house. They've been waiting for me.
STEVE TRENT:	Did you see them?
PAUL TEMPLE:	No. Now, Steve, listen. I'm going across the tennis court to the front of the drawing-room. They won't be able to see me from there. I shall be gone about two minutes. Keep the car running.
STEVE TRENT:	But – what are you going to do?
PAUL TEMPLE:	I – I can't explain now, Steve. But as soon as I get back to the car, let it rip!

STEVE TRENT:	Yes, yes, all right.

Incidental music.

SIR GRAHAM:	(*Fade in*) Well, I'm damned if I can understand it. We must have been here nearly two hours.
DALE:	Did Temple say he was coming back here, Sir Graham?
SIR GRAHAM:	Yes, of course he did, Dale! After the raid on the Inn, he'd have departed with Miss Parchment and said he'd meet us here, didn't he, Merritt?
MERRITT:	That's right, sir.
DALE:	Well, he wasn't at Ashdown House when I left.
SIR GRAHAM:	Of course he wasn't. What the devil would he be doing at Ashdown House?
MERRITT:	Well, wherever he is, I think he might have telephoned, instead of keeping us in the dark like this.
SIR GRAHAM:	Yes, I agree with you, Merritt.
DALE:	H'm. Well, look at this, Sir Graham. Perhaps this explains why we haven't received a telephone message!
SIR GRAHAM:	Good God!
MERRITT:	Why?
DALE:	The wire's been cut.
MERRITT:	But it can't have been! Unless …
SIR GRAHAM:	Unless what, Merritt?
MERRITT:	I was going to say … unless it's been done quite recently.
DALE:	I say, Sir Graham, do you know anything about this butler fellow – Pryce?

SIR GRAHAM:	No. No, I don't, Dale. And then there's the woman, er, the woman who says she's Steve Trent's landlady – Mrs Neddy. She's still in the house, remember.
DALE:	Yes, you're right, Sir Graham. And she delivered the gramophone record that time when Temple and Miss Trent had such –
MERRITT:	(*Interrupting*) You don't have to worry about Pryce, why he –

Suddenly a stone crashes through a window.

SIR GRAHAM:	Good God! What's that?
DALE:	A stone!
MERRITT:	It came through the French windows! Look! There it is.
DALE:	A stone! Why the devil should anyone – I say, look, there's a piece of paper wrapped round it.
MERRITT:	Aye, aye, it's a note.

A car engine revving up can be heard in the distance.

SIR GRAHAM:	Listen! Listen!
MERRITT:	Well, that's certainly a quick getaway. I say, I say, what does it say on the note?
DALE:	Yes. Yes. What is it, Sir Graham?
SIR GRAHAM:	Yes, er, just a second. Er, here we are …
DALE:	Well?
MERRITT:	What is it?
SIR GRAHAM:	It says, "Temple caught … First Penguin awaiting instructions … Malvern Pigeons despatched … Ludmilla."

END OF EPISODE SEVEN

EPISODE EIGHT

EXIT THE KNAVE

Announcements. Incidental music

SIR GRAHAM:	(*Fade in*) Well, I'm damned if I can understand it. We must have been here nearly two hours.
DALE:	Did Temple say he was coming back here, Sir Graham?
SIR GRAHAM:	Yes, of course he did, Dale! After the raid on the Inn, he departed with Miss Parchment and said he'd meet us here, didn't he, Merritt?
MERRITT:	That's right, sir.
DALE:	Well, he wasn't at Ashdown House when I left.
SIR GRAHAM:	Of course he wasn't. What the devil would he be doing at Ashdown House?
MERRITT:	Well, wherever he is, I think he might have telephoned, instead of keeping us in the dark like this.
SIR GRAHAM:	Yes, I agree with you, Merritt.
DALE:	H'm. Well, look at this, Sir Graham. Perhaps this explains why we haven't received a telephone message!
SIR GRAHAM:	Good God!
MERRITT:	Why?
DALE:	The wire's been cut.
MERRITT:	But it can't have been! Unless …
SIR GRAHAM:	Unless what, Merritt?
MERRITT:	I was going to say … unless it's been done quite recently.
DALE:	I say, Sir Graham, do you know anything about this butler fellow – Pryce?
SIR GRAHAM:	No. No, I don't, Dale. And then there's the woman, er, the woman who says she's

171

	Steve Trent's landlady – Mrs Neddy. She's still in the house, remember.
DALE:	Yes, you're right, Sir Graham. And she delivered the gramophone record that time when Temple and Miss Trent had such –
MERRITT:	(*Interrupting*) You don't have to worry about Pryce, why he –

Suddenly a stone crashes through a window.

SIR GRAHAM:	Good God! What's that?
DALE:	A stone!
MERRITT:	It came through the French windows! Look! There it is.
DALE:	A stone! Why the devil should anyone – I say, look, there's a piece of paper wrapped round it.
MERRITT:	Aye, aye, it's a note.

A car engine revving up can be heard in the distance.

SIR GRAHAM:	Listen! Listen!
MERRITT:	Well, that's certainly a quick getaway. I say, I say, what does it say on the note?
DALE:	Yes. Yes. What is it, Sir Graham?
SIR GRAHAM:	Just a second. Er, here we are …
DALE:	Well?
MERRITT:	What is it?
SIR GRAHAM:	It says, "Temple caught … First Penguin awaiting instructions … Malvern Pigeons despatched … Ludmilla."
MERRITT:	Temple caught!
DALE:	Ludmilla! Who the hell is Ludmilla?
SIR GRAHAM:	She's a friend of this man Max Lorraine, alias the Knave of Diamonds. She's the girl who lived at Ashdown House with this so-called Dr Milton.

DALE:	Oh, yes. But I say – who's the First Penguin?
SIR GRAHAM:	God knows! This business seems to get more complicated week after week.
MERRITT:	And what do they mean by "Malvern pigeons despatched"?
SIR GRAHAM:	There are some pigeons at The Little General. I wonder –
DALE:	(*Interrupting*) Good Lord, yes!
MERRITT:	Yes, of course. Of course, there are.
DALE:	Malvern … Malvern pigeons despatched … Why – why it must have some connections with the robbery at Malvern … Surely that's why –
MERRITT:	(*Interrupting*) Good Lord!
SIR GRAHAM:	What is it?
MERRITT:	We are damn fools if you like. That's how they've been getting the diamonds out of the country –
DALE:	You mean … by pigeons … carrier pigeons?
MERRITT:	Aye.
SIR GRAHAM:	Well, I'm damned!
MERRITT:	But, Sir Graham, why should they give the game away, in a note like this … "Malvern pigeons despatched." …They must have known we'd guess.
SIR GRAHAM:	They're not worried about our guessing their little secrets now, Merritt. All they're concerned about is getting the whole matter straightened out, and then vanishing. And, by Gad, it looks as if they're doing it … They've got Temple … and they've got the girl.

DALE:	Yes, but that still doesn't explain why this note was thrown through the window, Sir Graham. The note was obviously meant for the Knave of Diamonds.
MERRITT:	Aye, that's right.
DALE:	Then this girl – er –
SIR GRAHAM:	Ludmilla.
DALE:	… Ludmilla, must believe that the Knave is here. Here, in this house.
SIR GRAHAM:	But there isn't anyone here except us and –
DALE:	(*Interrupting*) And Pryce.
SIR GRAHAM:	Yes, and Pryce.
MERRITT:	Oh, but Pryce is out of the question, why – Just a minute! I say, just a minute! Don't forget that old woman's still here, Mrs Neddy.
SIR GRAHAM:	Steve Trent's landlady. H'm. I was forgetting her.
DALE:	The thing that really beats me is this First Penguin reference. What the devil, or who the devil, is the First Penguin?
MERRITT:	Aye, that's what I'd like to know.
DALE:	Can you think what they mean, sir?
SIR GRAHAM:	I'm damned if I can! I say, I hope Steve Trent and Temple are all right: if anything happens to them …
MERRITT:	Yes. Yes, I 'ope so too.
SIR GRAHAM:	Well, look here, it's no good staying here all night. I'm getting back to the Yard with the note. I'd like Henderson to have a look at it. He can make sense out of any damn thing.

174

DALE:	I'll pick Turner up at The Little General, then Mowbray and company at Ashdown House. Is that all right, Sir Graham?
SIR GRAHAM:	Yes. I should bring Turner back here and let him keep guard on the house. He might keep an eye on this fellow – er – Pryce.
DALE:	Yes.
MERRITT:	Well, I'm off back to Malvern. I left Sergeant Rogers there, and I'm just –

Door opens.

SIR GRAHAM:	Just a moment! Oh yes, Pryce, what is it?
PRYCE:	I beg your pardon, sir, but – er – Mrs Neddy would rather like to speak to you.
SIR GRAHAM:	Oh, yes, of course.
MRS NEDDY:	Excuse me, sir …
SIR GRAHAM:	What is it, Mrs Neddy?
MRS NEDDY:	Sorry to bother you now, sir, but I'm that worried, I am, about Miss Trent 'an I was wonderin' if you could –
SIR GRAHAM:	(*Interrupting*) Oh, I'm sorry, Mrs Neddy, but – er – well, so far we haven't any news.
MRS NEDDY:	Oh, dear, oh, dear.
SIR GRAHAM:	I'll see that a car is sent for you, Mrs Neddy, so that you can get back into town. As soon as we have any news, we'll let you know.
MRS NEDDY:	Thank you, sir. You're very kind, sir.
PRYCE:	Sorry to have troubled you, sir.
SIR GRAHAM:	Er - that's all right, Pryce. As a matter of fact, er, we're leaving. If, er, if by any chance you should hear from Mr Temple, ask him to get in touch with Scotland Yard. Whitehall 1212.

PRYCE: Whitehall 1212. Very good, sir.

Incidental music.

A car is heard pulling up.

MORRISON: The trouble with you, Miller, is that you don't treat this place as a police station. You act as if you were in a farmhouse.

PC MILLER: I'm very sorry, Sergeant.

MORRISON: Damn it, man, what's the use of being –

Door opens.

MORRISON: Ah, good evening, Mr Temple.

PAUL TEMPLE: Good evening, Sergeant. Evening, Miller.

PC MILLER: Good evening, sir.

MORRISON: Well, what can we do for you, Mr Temple?

PAUL TEMPLE: I'd like to have a word with you, Sergeant, if – er –

MORRISON: Yes, yes, of course. Right, Miller, you can go. Report to me again later, with Constable Hodges.

PC MILLER: Yes, sir.

Door closes.

PAUL TEMPLE: Sergeant, tell me, have you heard of a small Inn known as The First Penguin?

MORRISON: No, sir, I'm afraid I haven't. The First Penguin ... that's a new one on me.

PAUL TEMPLE: It's about four miles from Harvington, tucked away down one of the side roads that leads to the river. There's an A.A. box on the corner, and a milestone with a name on it that looks to me very much like Bidford.

MORRISON: Yes. Yes, I think I know that spot you mean now I come to think of it. I say, this

	First Penguin; it isn't that ramshackle-looking place with a grey roof –
PAUL TEMPLE:	Yes. Yes, that's right, Sergeant.
MORRISON:	H'm.
PAUL TEMPLE:	Now listen, I want you to get as many men as possible and have them stationed at the corner near the milestone. If anyone leaves The First Penguin and comes towards the main road, arrest them. No matter who, or what, they are. Arrest them! Is that clear, Sergeant?
MORRISON:	No matter … who … or what … they are?
PAUL TEMPLE:	(*Gravely*) Yes. Even if it's the Chief Commissioner himself!
MORRISON:	(*Laughs*) Well, I hardly expect that we shall find Sir Graham Forbes, Mr Temple.
PAUL TEMPLE:	You never know. You never know, Sergeant.
MORRISON:	H'm. Er – when would you like the men there. I'm afraid I –
PAUL TEMPLE:	(*Interrupting*) The sooner the better.
MORRISON:	Very well, Mr Temple. I'll do my best.
PAUL TEMPLE:	Keep the men well out of sight, and don't, under any circumstances interfere with anyone who looks like making their way towards the First Penguin. When you see a light in one of the windows – enter the Inn.
MORRISON:	Very good, sir. Er – Mr Temple, if it isn't a personal question, who do you think will visit the Inn tonight?
PAUL TEMPLE:	The Knave of Diamonds, Sergeant.

Pause.

DIANA: (*Fade in*) Can't you do anything except sit there and grumble? We must have been tied up here for hours, and all you've damned well done is –

DR MILTON: (*Interrupting*) For Heaven's sake, woman! Shut up!

DIANA: Well, something's got to be done one way or the other. We can't just … sit … Oh, God! … this is tight!

DR MILTON: It's no earthly use struggling.

DIANA: But, we must – they must get … Oh!

DR MILTON: It's no use, Diana!

DIANA: If I could only get this rope free at the back, I could … move my arms, and then …

DR MILTON: When I get my hands on that little swine Horace!

DIANA: I hope Horace caught Temple before he got to Bramley Lodge.

DR MILTON: I wonder what on earth made the Chief ring up from Temple's place! Now that was a damn' fool thing to do, if you like!

DIANA: Why was it? How was he to know Temple was here, and would trace the call?

DR MILTON: (*Suddenly*) I say, what was that?

DIANA: What? Listen …

DR MILTON: I thought –

A car is heard approaching outside.

DR MILTON: It's a car!

The squeal of car brakes.

DIANA: Yes! I hope to God it's the Chief.

Footsteps are heard approaching from outside.

The door opens.

DR MILTON: Temple!

PAUL TEMPLE: Yes, my dear Milton. You must forgive me for once again –

STEVE TRENT: Paul! Where's Miss Parchment?

PAUL TEMPLE: Yes. Yes. Where is she Milton? (*Pause*) Milton, if you don't –

DIANA: (*Interrupting*) She's gone. She left about an hour ago.

PAUL TEMPLE: Why? (*Urgently*) Why did she leave?

A pause.

PAUL TEMPLE: Well, perhaps it's a good job you don't feel like talking.

DR MILTON: What – what are you going to do?

PAUL TEMPLE: Just, erm, gag you, my friend. We don't want you to be unnecessarily noisy when our distinguished guest arrives. Here, you attend to the girl, Steve.

DIANA: Who … who's coming here?

PAUL TEMPLE: A friend of yours, Miss Thornley. A very close friend, if I'm not mistaken.

DIANA: Not … not … Max! No! No! No!

DIANA's voice fades as she is gagged.

PAUL TEMPLE: And now turn the light out, Steve.

The sound of the light switch.

PAUL TEMPLE: Good … And now … we wait.

Pause.

STEVE TRENT: (*With trepidation*) Paul … is he really coming here?

PAUL TEMPLE: Yes. Yes, I think so, Steve.

STEVE TRENT: You're not certain?

PAUL TEMPLE: One can never be too certain of people, least of all, people like Max Lorraine.

STEVE TRENT: But, Paul, why should he come here? For what –

179

PAUL TEMPLE: (*Interrupting*) Because I've laid a trap, Steve. A rather neat little trap, with –

STEVE TRENT: What is it?

A car is heard approaching outside.

PAUL TEMPLE: Listen!

The car breaks and comes to a stop.

STEVE TRENT: (*Slightly worried*) Paul! Paul he's here.

PAUL TEMPLE: By Timothy, yes! Steve, stand by the light. When I give the signal, switch it on.

STEVE TRENT: Yes … yes, all right.

PAUL TEMPLE: Quietly.

A pause.

Footsteps are heard approaching.

The door opens.

DALE: Ludmilla! Ludmilla! Ludmilla, where are you? Why don't you … Who's there?

PAUL TEMPLE: Lights, Steve!

The light switches on.

PAUL TEMPLE: Drop that gun!

The sound of a gun being dropped.

STEVE TRENT: Why – why it's Dale! Inspector Dale!

PAUL TEMPLE: Yes, Inspector Dale. Alias Max Lorraine, alias – The Knave of Diamonds!

DALE: Temple, are you mad? What the devil does this mean?

PAUL TEMPLE: Briefly, my dear Lorraine, it means, exit the Knave. Steve, ungag the girl.

DALE: Ludmilla, why did you send that note?

DIANA: Note? Which note?

DALE: Good God! You don't mean … Temple!

PAUL TEMPLE: (*With a chuckle*) Yes, I sent the note … my method of delivering it was a little unconventional, I admit. But it seems to have served its purpose.

DIANA:	You damned fool, Max! You played straight into his hands. Why –

The door opens again.
There are a lot of voices as several policemen enter.

MORRISON:	We saw the light, Mr Temple, and –
PAUL TEMPLE:	Yes. Ah, hello, Sir Graham, hello Charles!
SIR GRAHAM:	So, you've got Milton and – Dale!
MORRISON:	Yes.
SIR GRAHAM:	I don't mind telling you, Temple, that Merritt and I were staggered when the sergeant gave us your note, why –
PAUL TEMPLE:	(*Interrupting*) Yes, I expect you were, Sir Graham.
MERRITT:	Have you searched him?
PAUL TEMPLE:	Not yet, Charles.
MERRITT:	Right. Then we'll wait till we get him back to the station.
SIR GRAHAM:	Take Milton and the girl to the car, Sergeant.
MORRISON:	Yes, sir. Come along, Miller, give me a hand.
PC MILLER:	Right you are, Sergeant.
MORRISON:	You untie the girl.
PC MILLER:	Very well.
DR MILTON:	Well, they say, give a man plenty of rope and he'll hang himself. You've certainly made a pretty good job of it, Max!
MORRISON:	Come along, you!
DR MILTON:	Goodbye, Mr Temple. This time, I'm afraid, we shan't meet again.
MORRISON:	Bring the girl, too, Miller.
PC MILLER:	Yes, sir.
DIANA:	So … it's goodbye, Max.

181

DALE: Yes. Yes, it's goodbye. But – remember what I always said, Ludmilla. They won't take me! They won't take _me_!

PC MILLER: Come along, miss.

Door closes.

A pause.

DALE: Do you mind if I have a cigarette, Sir Graham?

SIR GRAHAM: Er, no, er, all right. You can have one of these.

DALE: If you don't mind, I'd rather not. I don't particularly care for your brand of Russian cigarettes. I have my own. You got a light, Merritt?

SIR GRAHAM: Yes, all right. Merritt.

A match is struck.

DALE: Ah, thank you. That's better.

MERRITT: Well, you've certainly given us plenty to think about, Dale.

SIR GRAHAM: Yes. But thank God we had the common sense to follow Miss Trent's advice and "Send for Paul Temple"!

MERRITT: I think we'll have the bracelets on, sir. Just to be on the safe side.

The sound of handcuffs being put on DALE.

DALE: Well, I've had a good run for my money. And I'm not grumbling. It's a pity you caught me on a cheap trick, Temple but – I guess that's how things turn out sometimes.

SIR GRAHAM: Dale, tell me … that time when Skid Tyler was poisoned. What happened?

DALE:	(*Chuckles*) The poison wasn't meant for Tyler. I can assure you of that, Sir Graham.
SIR GRAHAM:	(*Shocked*) Then – then it must have been meant for me!

DALE starts to laugh uncontrollably, then starts to cough.

SIR GRAHAM:	What the devil is it, Dale?
STEVE TRENT:	Paul! He's going to faint!
PAUL TEMPLE:	My God! It's the cigarette! He's poisoned himself!
DALE:	(*Still coughing*) I told Ludmilla … you'd never take me! (*Starts laughing again*)
PAUL TEMPLE:	(*Urgently*) Get him to the car, Merritt! Get him to the car!
MERRITT:	We'll have to get him into Evesham.

DALE falls to the ground.

MERRITT:	He's passed out. We'll have to be quick, Sir Graham!
SIR GRAHAM:	Yes. Here I … just a second … Just lift him … I'll give you a hand.
MERRITT:	(*Straining*) That's all right.
SIR GRAHAM:	Careful.

Door closes.

STEVE TRENT:	How horrible! Did you see his face? He was – oh, Paul!
PAUL TEMPLE:	Don't – my dear!
STEVE TRENT:	(*Pulling herself together*) Paul, why did the Knave come here? Did you know it was Dale, and why –
PAUL TEMPLE:	(*Chuckling*) One question at a time, Steve! I'd had my suspicions about Dale for quite a little while, and when I got back to Bramley Lodge and found that he'd been there all night and had had ample

opportunity of using the telephone, I was almost certain.

STEVE TRENT: But he wasn't the only person at Bramley Lodge.

PAUL TEMPLE: No. There was Sir Graham and Merritt. Sir Graham, of course, was really quite out of the question, although even with Sir Graham I found myself occasionally, well, wondering. I think it was those Russian cigarettes he smoked.

STEVE TRENT: But … there was Merritt?

PAUL TEMPLE: Yes, there was Merritt. And, quite frankly, it rather worried me. You see, Merritt was in Sir Graham's office the day Skid Tyler was murdered. Merritt knew that you were Louise Harvey … and he turned up tonight at The Little General when the Inn was raided.

STEVE TRENT: (*Thoughtfully*) Yes.

PAUL TEMPLE: And there was one other point, too. Merritt, apparently, according to Pryce, had used the telephone when Dale and Sir Graham had returned to The Little General. This seemed to fit perfectly, but still, somehow or other, I didn't think Merritt was our man.

STEVE TRENT: But – but when did Dale phone?

PAUL TEMPLE: After Sir Graham and Merritt returned to Bramley Lodge from the Inn, two of them went down to Ashdown House. Unfortunately, Pryce wasn't sure which two. We know now, of course, that it must have been Merritt and Sir Graham. It was then that Dale took the opportunity of

184

ringing through here … to see if Milton and the gang had got clear with the Malvern diamonds.

STEVE TRENT: Yes. But I still don't see how you managed to trick Dale –

PAUL TEMPLE: (*Interrupting*) I'm coming to that, Steve. When I got back to the house and discovered that Sir Graham, Merritt, and Dale were in the drawing-room, I decided to find out, once and for all, who was the Knave. I scribbled a short note which said, "Temple caught. First Penguin awaiting instructions. Malvern pigeons despatched. Ludmilla." This I pitched through the drawing-room window. Now the note would, I felt sure, read like utter nonsense to anyone in that room, except, of course, Max Lorraine. And Lorraine would, I felt confident, immediately assume that Temple had been caught and that Milton and Ludmilla, alias Diana Thornley, were waiting for him at The First Penguin.

STEVE TRENT: Yes, yes, I see.

PAUL TEMPLE: The phrase, "First Penguin awaiting instructions" would, of course, sound like the most utter balderdash to Sir Graham and Merritt, who wouldn't even know what The First Penguin stood for. Dale knew perfectly well what the note meant, however, and acted accordingly.

STEVE TRENT: But … what did you mean by "Malvern pigeons despatched"?

PAUL TEMPLE: Ah, yes. You remember I went round to the courtyard just before we were due to leave for Bramley Lodge?

STEVE TRENT: Yes – that was after you noticed the pigeons.

PAUL TEMPLE: That's right. Well, in the courtyard was a basket of pigeons obviously all ready to carry the Malvern diamonds to their destination. That's how they've been getting the stuff out of the country, Steve, by carrier pigeon.

STEVE TRENT: That's ingenious, if you like!

PAUL TEMPLE: Yes. And a reference to it in the note, which was, of course, supposed to come from Diana Thornley, alias Ludmilla, would, I thought, give the note an authentic touch. When I got down to the station, Sergeant Morrison informed me that earlier in the evening Merritt had been through on the phone from Bramley Lodge to see if Morrison had seen or heard anything about Miss Parchment and myself. This, of course, accounted for the telephone call that Merritt had made, and to a very large extent cleared him of suspicion. While I was at the station, I wrote another note, which I addressed to Sir Graham and left with the Sergeant, on the strict understanding that he would deliver it to Sir Graham <u>only</u> if the Chief Commissioner arrived at the police station accompanied by Merritt. The note, of course, expressed my opinion about Dale being Max Lorraine. The Knave would, I

186

	felt positive, get to The First Penguin as quickly as possible in accordance with the instructions on my first note.
STEVE TRENT:	Well, you certainly seem to have been exploiting your literary …

The door opens.

PAUL TEMPLE:	Hello, Charles, what is it?
MERRITT:	He's … he's dead, Paul.
STEVE TRENT:	Dead?
PAUL TEMPLE:	I see.
MERRITT:	I felt p'rhaps you'd rather like to know.
PAUL TEMPLE:	Yes! Yes, of course. Thank you, Charles.
MERRITT:	Well, personally, I can't say I'm sorry this business is over. It certainly put the wind up me!
PAUL TEMPLE:	W–why do you say that?
MERRITT:	Well, as a matter of fact, Paul, I have literally been quivering in ma shoes since the first day I heard about the Knave of Diamonds.
PAUL TEMPLE:	Yes, but why?
MERRITT:	When I was a small and rather energetic youngster of about nine, I fell off a tricycle, Paul. It made a scar – a rather small scar – about the right elbow.
PAUL TEMPLE:	Oh!

STEVE starts to laugh loudly.

PAUL TEMPLE:	(*Chuckling*) Oh! Oh, I see.

Both STEVE and PAUL laugh loudly.

MERRITT:	(*Not sharing the joke*) I'll see you both later at Bramley Lodge.

STEVE and PAUL continue to laugh.

Door closes.

STEVE TRENT:	Perhaps, in a way, Paul, it's for the best.

PAUL TEMPLE:	Yes. Yes, perhaps it is, Steve.
STEVE TRENT:	Well … this brings us to the end of our little adventure.
PAUL TEMPLE:	Yes, I'm afraid it does. Exit the Knave.
STEVE TRENT:	I want to get back to Town as quickly as possible, this story's rather important –
PAUL TEMPLE:	Steve …
STEVE TRENT:	Yes?
PAUL TEMPLE:	I was wondering if you, erm …
STEVE TRENT:	Well?
PAUL TEMPLE:	If you'd – er – care to have dinner with me on … on Thursday?
STEVE TRENT:	Thursday? Oh, yes, of course. I'd love to.
PAUL TEMPLE:	Good. I shall be in town, so perhaps we can … er … lunch together, too?
STEVE TRENT:	Yes. Why not?
PAUL TEMPLE:	We might even manage to have tea together, as a sort of, – a sort of er –
STEVE TRENT:	I'd love to.
PAUL TEMPLE:	Oh, er, splendid. Well, that's about all. Of course, there is breakfast, but –
STEVE TRENT:	(*Interrupting*) I always have breakfast in bed.
PAUL TEMPLE:	In bed?
STEVE TRENT:	Yes.
PAUL TEMPLE:	Oh … erm … well, that's a bit awkward.
STEVE TRENT:	Of course, we could get married.
PAUL TEMPLE:	Yes, I suppose so. There would be some difficulty – I – I say! I say, are you proposing?
STEVE TRENT:	What do you think, Mr Temple? What do you think?
PAUL TEMPLE:	(*Laughing*) Well, of all the unconventional little devils, you simply –

A loud banging noise is heard.

STEVE TRENT: (*Shocked; surprised*) What's that?

PAUL TEMPLE: It's from the cupboard!

STEVE TRENT: Yes! Yes, what is it?

PAUL TEMPLE: We'll soon find out. Stand on one side, Steve. (*With authority*) Stand on one side!

The cupboard door is opened.

PAUL TEMPLE: Why – why, it's Miss Parchment!

STEVE TRENT: Miss Parchment!

MISS PARCHMENT: Give me some air! Where's Dr Milton and the girl?

PAUL TEMPLE: They've gone, Miss Parchment.

MISS PARCHMENT: Gone?

PAUL TEMPLE: They've been arrested. And the Knave's gone, too. He's dead. It was Dale – Inspector Dale, of Scotland Yard.

MISS PARCHMENT: You mean to say that all this has been going on while I've been in that blasted cupboard?

PAUL TEMPLE: Yes.

MISS PARCHMENT: Well! By Timothy!

THE END

Meet Paul Temple

Francis Durbridge tells how he came into existence

The introduction of a new and rather unusual character to listeners is always something of a gamble, but Paul Temple made his debut in a rather delightful and encouraging atmosphere of 'big things to come'.

I am glad to say some of the 'big things' have already materialised. The novel *Send for Paul Temple*, which, oddly enough, was written *after* the radio play, not before as is usually the case, is shortly to be published.

During the past two months so much has been written about the character of Paul Temple, that I feel almost reluctant to add further details. Indeed, I would not do so if it were not that in every letter I have received about the serial (even the rude ones) there had been a polite inquiry where, and in what circumstances, I first met Paul Temple. This determination on the part of the listeners to look upon Temple as a human being has no doubt been largely due to the spirited performance of the artist playing the part and to the fact that, with the rest of the cast, he is to remain anonymous until the end of the serial.

Contrary to general opinion, however, one does not take a character from life and insert him boldly in a novel or play, for apart from the law of libel the character would oddly enough, very soon cease to convince. On the other hand, a character can most certainly be suggested by a living person, for without this suggestion one cannot possibly hope to create the illusion of reality.

I had been thinking about a principal character for my serial thriller for almost three months before I actually came across the person whose manner, voice, and attitude suggested to me the man-of-the-world novelist with an active interest in criminology.

I had discussed several characters I had in mind with Martyn C. Webster, the producer, but they seemed rather indifferent and vague, and we both agreed that the thriller needed a definite character with a name that listeners would like and readily remember. At length we settled on the name 'Paul Temple', although 'Mark Conway' ran it a very close second. But having settled on the name I still had to draw the character, and before doing so felt that I should have to meet someone whose manner and appearance would suggest a definite train of thought. At all cost Paul Temple must be made to sound like a human being and not merely a mixture of Bulldog Drummond and Tiger Standish.

At first I visualised Temple as a rather bright young police officer straight from the training college, but somehow the character did not appeal to me like this and I felt sure the listeners would merely look upon him as a juvenile Hornleigh. Secondly, I visualised Temple as a middle-aged doctor with an unusual flair for putting two and two together, but the producer quite rightly felt that a middle-aged doctor would appear to listeners as a counterpart of the famous Dr Watson.

Then I went to London for a few days and on the day I was returning to Birmingham I arrived at the station, with hardly a minute to spare. The train was, in fact, already moving when I stumbled into the last compartment. There was one other occupant of the carriage and he slowly raised his head at my unexpected entrance. As far as I can remember he was short and dark, and was reading a battered copy of Arnold Bennett's *Imperial Palace*. I exclaimed, "Better late than never!" To which he replied in a rather charming voice, "Yes, better late than never." We never spoke again.

Now for some unknown reason, after he had left the train, I started thinking about him. I remembered the manner in which he had inserted a cigarette in an unusual type of holder, and the careless – yet not patronising – indifference with which he displayed his season ticket. And the man had other characteristics which fascinated me. I felt sure that here, at last, was the necessary background upon which to develop Paul Temple. The man in the train was obviously interested in literature and not merely a casual reader; one could tell that by the way he pondered over the novel he was reading. This made me think that he might possibly be a novelist, although I had to admit his face was not familiar.

However, I saw no reason why Temple shouldn't be a novelist and a very popular one into the bargain!

Outwardly, I am afraid Temple bears very little resemblance to the man in the train. He is tall and fair, whereas my travelling companion was dark and on the short side. But had I missed that train there is a possibility that Paul Temple might have made his debut on the air as a rather clerical-looking little man with a passion for criminology and a complete indifference to Steve Trent. By Timothy!

Press Pack

Press cuttings about Send For Paul Temple …

BBC Will Keep Names Secret In Serial Thriller

Meet Paul Temple. He is 38, lives near Evesham. Educated at Rugby and Magdalen College, Oxford. Successful mystery novelist, less successful playwright. Known to many as a criminologist.

Paul Temple is the sleuth whom Francis Durbridge has called in to solve a series of baffling jewel robberies due in the Midlands in early April.

They are to form the subject of a serial thriller. One episode a week, lasting about twenty-five minutes, will be broadcast starting on 8 April. It is reckoned that once you get caught up with the sinister business you will be on tenterhooks until the next Friday comes round. And having read the first episode (entitled *"The Green Finger"*) I am inclined to agree that anyone who hears that will make arrangements to be within earshot of a radio set for the seven succeeding Friday nights.

It's all set in the Midlands. A good kick-off with an £8,000 haul of diamonds in Birmingham, then the action shoots down to Worcestershire and – well, you never know when the centre of things will be in YOUR home town.

The Jewellers' Association have helped with the preparation of the script and author Francis Durbridge has also been consulting with the C.I.D. getting details right.

Actually there will be two mysteries to keep you guessing. Apart from the plot and the identity of "Paul Temple" the others taking part will be kept a secret until the very end.

Meet "Paul Temple"

The new Midland serial detective thriller, which, as I announced a fortnight ago, is to start in April, has been given the title, "*Send For Paul Temple.*" Needless to add, Paul Temple is the name of the super amateur sleuth who is to conduct us through the Midland underworld. He will be found up against a band of international crooks of great subtlety and almost infinite resource. Mr Francis Durbridge's story will run, I am told, to about eight instalments; but probably by the time we have followed his exploits through this initial series of bafflers we shall be ripe for more. Then will be the time to "Send for Mr Durbridge."

One who has read the scripts confides that Temple is more like Dorothy Sayers' delightful Lord Peter Wimsey than Sherlock Holmes or Inspector Hornleigh. But that is not to say that he owes anything to anybody in the matter of personality and technique. It will be interesting to know who will interpret him.

This Secret Of the BBC Is A Secret　　Gordon Robinson

If, during the next few days, you see a mysterious-looking gent with coat collar turned up, hat pulled down over his eyes, creeping furtively into the Midland studios, don't leap to the conclusion that it's burglars.

Ten to one it will be Mr Paul Temple trying to avoid recognition.

The identity of Midland's new radio serial sleuth is a Secret of the BBC that even Mr Michie can't tell you.

Even other performers in the radio serial which is to start on Friday didn't know until they turned up for rehearsals today who was to take the name part. Listeners won't discover his identity (unless they find it out for themselves) until the serial finishes in two months' time.

To help readers of the *Despatch* I've secured the first photograph of Paul Temple to appear in the press in this country. It only shows his shadow I'm afraid, but on Friday you'll have the voice (which you've heard often before) as an additional clue. Drop me a line if you think you recognise it.

Good sign of the listener-interest that Paul Temple should arouse is the fact that artists taking part are themselves getting all keyed up about the mystery. So far they've only had the scripts of the early episodes, and they're getting impatient to find out what the end is going to be.

Send for Paul Temple!

The first episode of a serial thriller, in which Paul Temple encounters the mystery of "*The Green Finger*" starts tonight at 8pm.

Francis Durbridge is known to radio listeners as the author of *Promotion*, *Murder at the Embassy*, and many other radio plays and light productions. The plot of *Send for Paul Temple!* involves a series of daring jewel robberies (imaginary of course) at various mansions in the Midlands, mysteries that the ingenious detective, Paul Temple, sets out to solve.

All the players engaged in this serial will remain anonymous.

Radio Sleuth, temperature 102, goes on with the show
Gordon Robinson

Paul Temple, Midland radio 'tec who faces death once weekly for your amusement, showed last night that he's tough in real life as well as in the thriller serial.

The actor who plays Mr Temple (you'll know his name in a fortnight's time) went through with the broadcast in spite of a temperature of 102 and in spite of feeling like one of the corpses which Mr Durbridge provides so liberally throughout the script.

Mr Temple's finger may, perhaps, have trembled on the trigger of his revolver – we didn't see it, but from his voice no one would have guessed that he was a sick man. The way in which he dealt with the dreadful doctor left me, at any rate, with undiminished confidence in his ability to rid the Midlands of its Vast Criminal Organisation.

BBC Rob Shopworkers of Weekly Thrill

Shop assistants are on the warpath. And they have good reason for any storm they stir up over the latest offence of the BBC.

It's like this.

Every Friday night for six weeks past at 9 or 9.30 Midland Regional listeners have been treated to half an hour's pleasurable excitement – to wit, an episode of the thriller serial "*Send for Paul Temple*." (Can't keep that name out of this column).

For those who have been following it, excitement is reaching fever pitch. Only two more instalments to go and the Knave of Diamonds is still at large.

So what do the BBC do? They calmly transfer this week's instalment to an earlier hour, when thousands of listeners – particularly those who work in shops – won't be able to hear it. This Friday Paul Temple is due to come on air at 7.30.

A number of shop assistants have, I believe, voiced a protest to the BBC. It won't induce the BBC to change their mind, I fear. All the same, it wouldn't do any harm if more of you who are upset by the new arrangement let the BBC know what you think. Politely if possible, but let them know anyway. For Friday evening offers a prize example of what goes by the name of Programme Planning.

Paul Temple already caters pretty well on Friday evenings for those who like thrills.

But the BBC chose this one evening of the week to put on as well a full-length thriller – Emlyn Williams' spine-chiller "*Night Must Fall*."

That occupies an hour-and-a-quarter – from 8.45 to 10.00. "*Paul Temple*," as I have said, is squeezed back to 7.35, and in between we have 45 minutes' motets and organ music by Mr Brahms. I've nothing against Mr Brahms, mind you. But motets don't stir the blood like the sound of bodies dropping into the Severn.

Local School "Send for Paul Temple"

Next Friday's instalment of "*Send For Paul Temple*" promises to be an exciting one. Up at Broadcasting House they've been firing bullets through windscreens to get the right sound effects (they'll be lamming a soprano if you're not careful). And a few days ago an expedition was made to Blue Coat School in Birmingham, where thrilling car chases were recorded.

It took most of the morning and an afternoon, because when everything was going fine some noise that wasn't wanted would make itself heard. The first time it was a passing cyclist. Then it was the birds (Yes, I'm not joking). And then it was an aeroplane.

They did their best, but I believe it's still possible that you'll hear the birds if you listen carefully.

Find The Knave

When they reveal the identity of the Knave of Diamonds at the end of the final episode of "*Send for Paul Temple*," on Friday evening, listeners won't be the only people with bated breath.

You see, the cast, although they are naturally aware of each other's identity, still don't know who is the Knave of Diamonds, head of the jewel thief gang. The idea behind this was to keep the actors as well as listeners keyed up …

The fact is, in confidence, most of the cast have had a little flutter on the Knave of Diamonds. They got a sweepstake together last weekend backing their fancy.

Maybe you'd like to have a shot, too? … Who is the Knave of Diamonds? Drop me a card with your solution on. All for fun. No prizes.

And Finally …

And so they found the Knave of Diamonds …

The final episode of "*Send for Paul Temple*" last night was as thrilling as all the others have been, plus … And it was as thrilling for players as the listeners. The Knave of Diamonds was, as you heard last night, none other than Inspector Dale. Nobody guessed of those who wrote to me, which is no cause for surprise, since Vincent Curran who played the part, didn't know until Thursday's rehearsal!

"Last week I had just a suspicion things were pointing towards me," he told me last night.

Actually, Vincent Curran, kind-eyed, greyish haired, thinning on top, is the least knavish-looking gentleman of the bunch … looks, in fact, like a schoolmaster. He lives in quiet Water Orton.

Curran, by the way, took part in the first night broadcast from Midland Regional, when the station was at Witton, way back in 1922.

It was in a thriller …

However, there is the merest suspicion of knavery afoot. You see, in the sweepstake, which I told you on Wednesday, the cast had run about the identity of the Knave, Vincent

200

Curran drew – Vincent Curran. Still he argues he thought he had backed a loser …

The serial, radio hit of the Midland Regional season so far, was a success for players, producer Martyn C. Webster, and 25-year-old Francis Durbridge, the Birmingham-born author.

Webster is so bucked, in fact, that he tells me he is seriously considering a sequel, maybe several. He'd be glad to know what you think of another Paul Temple. Drop him a line …

Author Durbridge is toying with the idea of writing another Paul Temple mystery, too. Meanwhile, he's pretty busy. Next months he's bringing out a book "*Send for Paul Temple.*" …

The rest of the time he's considering piles of offers for film and stage rights for the play. Yesterday he signed an option with a film company, the name of which we cannot divulge at the moment …

When it was all over gangsters and others partook themselves across the way where, in a room murky with flickering candles in bottles, and gruesomely decorated walls, the Knave broke bread with those whom he had deceived …

Success of Paul Temple

As an instance of the way listeners will respond when they are really interested, I might cite the enormous correspondence which has poured into the Broad Street offices of Midland Region since the broadcasting last Friday night of the eighth and final episode in the Paul Temple serial. Listeners were invited to drop a line to the BBC – if only a post card – saying if they had enjoyed this first Midland serial, and would like something of the sort again. I gather that the result has been the biggest letter-bag which any

Midland feature has yet earned – and it is virtually unanimous in its warm approval.

Mr Francis Durbridge, the Birmingham author, wrote the Paul Temple serial as a series of eight complete episodes, with recurrent characters, but early on I ventured to suggest that the idea and its execution was so admirable as almost to make certain a demand for its extension. It is too early to say what will be done, but I gather that Mr Durbridge is about to be called into consultation again – and his vivid and fertile mind should find no difficulty in either continuing the same series (the preferable course, I feel), or devising another. Paul Temple, as an amateur detective, is fit company for his contemporaries in modern fiction, and should not merely be faded off the ether, on to the printed page of Mr Durbridge's book.

The Public Asks For More Paul Temple

At the end of the final instalment of Midland's "Send for Paul Temple," Martyn C. Webster asked people to send in postcards saying whether they wanted more or less of Paul Temple.

Within 24 hours nearly 5,000 letters and postcards were received at the Broad Street Studios from all over the country; the number to date is about 6,000, the great many of them bearing the request, "More Paul Temple, please."

For the benefit of those who missed the announcement of the cast, The Knave, alias Max Lorraine, was played by Vincent Curran, and the mysterious Miss Parchment by Courtney Hope, who does so much good work.

It was a pity that the career of Inspector Harvey, who was murdered right at the beginning of the play, was played by Duncan Blyth, acting manager of the Birmingham Crescent Theatre, gave small scope to any actor.

Midland Drama Plans

The Midland serial thriller "*Send for Paul Temple*" drew over 7,500 letters of appreciation from listeners. Martyn C. Webster, who produced the play, is arranging for another thriller to run through the winter months. Francis Durbridge will again be the author, and the story will centre round the detective Paul Temple. The exact date for the second story to begin is not yet fixed.